# BY THE RIVER
## 1840-1899

JAE CARVEL

COPYRIGHT 2015 JAE CARVEL

Cover Design by Tatiana Vila
Edited by Mary Resk
Drawings by Jane Walter Bousman

*This is a work of fiction. Names, characters, places, brands, media, and incidents are either the product of the author's imagination or are used fictitiously. Any resemblance to similarly named places or to persons living or deceased is unintentional.*

Library of Congress Control Number:
2015903367

*This book is dedicated to the pioneers from the Manwaring Wagon Train and the Monday Authors who meet at my kitchen table.*

# PART I

# FISHING POLES AND MEMORIES
## AUGUST 1870

**"MAMA! LINCOLN FELL IN!"** yelled J.J.

Sarah Ann sprang from the bank and waded into the John Day River to rescue four-year-old Lincoln as he splashed and gulped the river water, fishing pole still grasped in his sturdy hand. J.J.'s annoyance at the attention Lincoln received spread across his face as he watched his mother rescue his little brother. With three precarious steps, Sarah Ann's everyday skirt became soaked up to her knees. As Lincoln sat on the riverbank to dry out, J.J. viewed the typical scene of his little brother garnering attention from their mother. This is how it had been since their father disappeared near Laramie on their way west. Lincoln got all the attention and J.J. was expected to be the "brave little man." He stomped through the brush to a better fishing hole, an eight-year-old man determined to get trout for breakfast.

Sarah Ann watched J.J. leave their chosen spot. "He is big enough not to fall in," she muttered under her breath. "I know I depend on him to be responsible, always have since our tragedy on the trail. Now that Thomas is his new stepfather, he is frustrated at being told what to do."

He was soon out of sight. Swirling pools ate away at the banks of the John Day River. Apprehension ate away at Sarah Ann's confidence in her son. She wrung the water from her skirt and used her light jacket to towel off Lincoln and thought, "J.J. has been out of sight too long."

"J.J., come back now, right now!" Her order went unanswered. She grabbed Lincoln by the arm and dragged him through the brush as fast as his wet little legs could carry him. She had to find J.J. and make sure he was all right. Wet, worried, and hindered by Lincoln, Sarah Ann felt panic creeping to a lump in her throat as branches snagged her skirt and scratched at her ankles. Then she spotted him just ahead, concentrating on his fishing line. She and Lincoln stopped and watched silently as J.J. netted a good-sized trout, hit the fish's head on a rock, and then strung him on the forked stick lying beside his pole.

"I'll be good and very quiet if you let me fish with you," promised Lincoln as he rushed over to J.J. Sarah Ann saw the boys come to agreement so she returned to her spot on the bank to let her skirts dry.

There were few days when Sarah Ann Martin found time to reminisce, but this seemed to be one of those rare times. A year ago, Sarah Ann had monitored her boys fishing on Dakota Creek as it gurgled near the Manwaring farm in Illinois. Today she sat by the John Day River in Oregon, ten miles from the headwaters that tumbled carelessly from the Blue Mountains. The river's pure water flowed over its gravelly bottom and swept near their homestead's well. Her boys managed to only occasionally get their lines tangled in the brush that shaded the inky deep pools where trout cavorted. Sarah Ann, the rancher's wife, sensed that her life was at last in order.

She remembered what brought her to the time when the Manwaring wagon train rolled from Edgewood, Illinois,

April 12, 1869. Supplies purchased from the sale of Captain Manwaring's farm and butcher shop crammed the wagons.

Manwaring husbands, wives, children, and grandchildren comprised the majority of the group. Cody and Sarah Ann Hunt Manwaring with their three children, J.J., Amy, and Lincoln, snuggled into their own wagon.

The Manwaring pioneer spirit, like lubricating grease, slid around in her husband Cody's mind. It glued his dream of being back in a saddle heading west to his very soul. Sarah Ann, who pursed the lips of her straight-across-the-face mouth, kept quiet about what she considered a reckless adventure. A month later the price she paid for her silence was far too high.

The Manwaring train was setting camp early one day in preparation for a long haul toward the Platte crossing. Some younger boys spotted antelope in the distance. Their shouts alerted the men who mounted up and headed for a kill. Captain spotted something else in the distance. Realizing it was a band of Indians, he yelled, "Riders ho! Circle up, circle up!" Cody did not hear or heed the call and rode on, rifle ready. The Indians, the antelope, and Cody disappeared over the horizon. Sarah Ann and her in-laws prayed through the long night and the next day as the men from the train searched as far as a day's ride could take them.

Nothing. They camped and searched, anguished and discouraged, for two weeks. Soldiers from Laramie found no trace of Cody, and the Manwaring train moved on without him. Her heart breaking from uncertainty, her grieving soul laced with hope, the widow and her children loaded up and moved ahead, one weary day at a time. Week after week the Manwarings mourned the loss of Cody. Captain continued to grimly direct the wagons. Mom Manwaring carried a silent sadness in her heart. Cody's sister, Kate, cried with the drama and passion of a sixteen-year-old. Crying was a luxury Sarah Ann did not allow herself. Sarah Ann's typically straight mouth was stone.

On rare occasions the boys or Amy would bring a smile to her eyes, but only to the grey eyes, never to the stoic lips. The men in the train helped her with the wagon, driving it through dangerous crossings of rivers and mountains, until they reached the tollgate crossing into Oregon's John Day Valley.

Sickness accompanied the weary travelers into the valley. Mom Manwaring and Sister Kate were taken in at the John Dearborn place, a homestead at the east end of the valley, where they were nursed back to health. The rest of the pioneers began the search for land to call their own. Sarah Ann and her children journeyed another thirteen miles to Prairie City. Instead of a hopeful family eager for new beginnings, they had been reduced to just a grim widow with three children to feed.

That was the day Thomas Martin rode to town for supplies. Going to town took half a day by the time he hitched the team, wrote out his supply list to be filled at Marsh's General Store, and allowed some time to jaw with town folk and patrons who stopped to sit a spell in front of the store. Thomas Martin, Matt Walter, and Will Stone shared a homestead three miles upriver. Thomas had carved his name at Council Bluff five years earlier on his way from Missouri to Oregon. His years of homesteading with Matt and Will had produced a ranch for one hundred head of white-faced cattle, with hay for winter and pasture for summer. The two-story log and lumber house testified to their carpentry skills. Eight thriving apple trees and a big garden distinguished them as good farmers. However, none of the three bachelors claimed to be a cook or housekeeper. Thomas had drawn supply duty for today, a task he rather enjoyed. Gossip of the newly arrived Manwaring train filled the air in town as Thomas tied his team and took a seat on the long bench in front of Marsh's.

Sarah Ann pulled her wagon to a halt, left J.J. to hold the reins, and climbed down. She walked in the front door of the general store and boldly asked, "Pardon me, do you know of boarding rooms or other places where I could make arrangements for my children and me to stay?" Marsh eyed the weary woman and pointed her to a bulletin board with its few scattered notices. Her entry did not go unnoticed by the few men outside the store. Thomas, whose ear was always cocked for news of good land deals, found himself listening to Sarah Ann as she queried the storekeeper. He also noticed the children in her wagon. They looked tired and thirsty. Thomas drew a dipper of water from Marsh's pump and offered drinks. His quiet manner appealed to Amy and Lincoln, and Sarah Ann came out to find him talking to the children and offering them each a piece of hard candy from the front pocket of his bib overalls.

"Howdy, Ma'am."

"Good day to you, Sir."

"My name is Thomas Martin and I have a good-sized place about three miles upriver that I share with my partners. I think I could offer you and your family room and board in exchange for cooking and housekeeping." Thomas knew it was impulsive and uncharacteristic of him to make the offer. He watched her face as she paused to think a moment. Her lips were moving, and under his breath he whispered, "Oh, my gosh, she accepted."

Scratching his long beard as he drove home, he wondered how to convince Matt and Will that hiring Sarah Ann was a wise decision. Shy Thomas deserved the ribbing he expected to get for grabbing a single lady with three young'uns along with the flour, baking powder, and other necessities from Marsh's. Following in her wagon, Sarah Ann wondered if she had been "swept off her feet" like the heroines of the novels she used to read as a girl in New York, or was she just grateful, so grateful …

They both pulled their wagons to a halt in front of the house. Four steps led to the front room with its chairs and a fireplace. Behind to the right was the downstairs bedroom. Sarah Ann thought it belonged to Thomas. The kitchen on the left was large and square with a wood range and a table in the middle. This was a palace compared to being crammed into a covered wagon for months. Sarah Ann was offered a bedroom upstairs for herself, Amy, and Lincoln.

J.J. commandeered an alcove to the right of the fireplace partly under the stairs. Matt and Will offered to bunk together in one room upstairs, a nice exchange for being excused from their cooking responsibilities.

A woman and three children in the house brought some changes. The men would hear, "J.J., Lincoln, wipe those feet!" and "Amy, get away from that stove." Hearty hot meals at noon and at the end of a day's work compensated for the requirement that Will move his tobacco spit bucket to the porch.

By winter the men decided to split the homestead, a plan that had always been part of their agreement. In Western tradition (one draws the boundaries and the others pick first) Matt drew the lines. Will chose the first piece of land, and Thomas paid some cash to keep the house and land where Jeff Davis Creek ran into the John Day River. Sarah Ann slipped into the equation as a willing worker, a grateful houseguest, and an intelligent companion. As the memories of her first husband, Cody Manwaring, slowly faded, Thomas Martin loomed near, patient and present, sharing his dreams for the future.

Sarah Ann and Thomas made a decision. One very chilly day in February, they bundled into the buckboard and drove the good team of Blackie and Mag fifteen miles to Canyon City, where the Grant County Judge, poet Joaquin Miller, married them. With some flamboyance he announced, "… Now I present Mr. and Mrs. Thomas Martin, husband and wife from the Martin Ranch in the upper valley of the John Day River!"

Sarah Ann was cursed with a mouth that rarely smiled. Her wedding day was no exception. She knew that some folks in Prairie City joked that Cody Manwaring rode off after antelope and never came back just to get away from her stern disposition. But that former life was now tucked away with the treasured perfume bottle her mother had given her when she left New York, in the back corner of the top dresser drawer. She closed her eyes and scooted across the buckboard seat next to Thomas for warmth and comfort on their ride home.

\* \* \*

Sarah Ann heard someone approaching and was jolted back to the reality of the everyday ranch life.

"Well, what have we here?" sounded the familiar voice of Thomas. "Amy and I happened upon some fishermen up the river a ways. Looks to me like they need the gunny sack their mother is guarding to carry home their catch."

Sarah Ann sighed as she responded, "Well, here it is." She looked at the three men in her life. "We better get back to the house. I can tell your sister Amy is wondering if she is going have trout to eat. Thomas, it's so nice you will be on hand to get all those fish cleaned properly with the heads removed!"

# TWO CRADLES
# NOVEMBER 1870

**THE MARTINS NEEDED** two cradles in their house. Thomas had built one as he and Sarah Ann awaited the birth of their first child. A blustery November thirtieth greeted a husky baby with a loud squall. Mom Manwaring came to help, and as evening approached Thomas heard her say, "Oh, my! Bring another baby blanket." A second baby entered the world. Twin boys nestled on either side of Sarah Ann in the bed she usually shared only with Thomas.

The next day Thomas harnessed the team and took the wagon down to the Foster place. "Art, I've come a-borrowing," he said hesitantly. He had grown up with his mother's admonition to never a borrower nor lender be. "Sarah Ann birthed twins last night and I need some time to make another cradle."

Art grabbed his hand in congratulations. Two weather-worn rough hands squeezed hard; words were unnecessary.

Scarred from cuts, rough from outdoor work in cold weather, the hands of two homesteaders did the speaking. Art produced a baby bed from under the side porch, a cast-off little bed from Art and Angie's first-born baby who did not survive the winter of '69. Angie was expecting again but refused to get baby gear ready ahead of time. Thomas figured the loan of the little bed would give him time to make a second cradle for his second boy.

"It needs some cleaning up." Art brushed away some cobwebs with his cracked knuckles. He and Thomas carried it to the wagon. "Come in and give Angie the news. She'll be pleased for you." Thomas felt ill at ease intruding, but Art was right.

Angie gave him a big smile and a little hug. "Take this extra loaf home to Sarah Ann for your dinner. Is Mom Manwaring staying with you?"

"For a couple of days Then Amy will help her ma and we'll get by. Much obliged for the bread."

Thomas and Art walked out to the wagon. "I'll get the bed back soon. I know you'll need it. I can probably make another cradle in a couple of weeks."

"No rush. Angie's due in January. Tell Sarah Ann we'll come calling next week and see those boys."

Thomas mounted the buckboard, clucked to the team, and decided to head on into Prairie City for some supplies. He knew they were low on flour and he wanted some finishing nails for the new cradle. He rarely shopped at Marsh's store without a list; it was always hard to think things out without a plan. Two baby boys. Definitely not in the plan. The wagon trip to town had given him some time to reminisce. Thomas had married Sarah Ann last winter after she and her three children had come to keep house for him. Their trip west in the Manwaring wagon train had landed her in Prairie City, a widow with one wagon and three children.

Thomas, a bearded bachelor, was smitten. Sarah Ann was an answer to his prayers. He, an answer to hers. Even acting as father to J. J., Amy, and Lincoln had not thrown him for a loop. As the oldest in his own family, Thomas had grown up caring for younger kids. But, two more children, immediate children, stretched his imagination, forced him to make necessary plans. He mulled over how to expand their full house as he stopped at Marsh's.

"I guess my chest is pumped up a bit," he heard himself saying to Marsh. "Sarah Ann had twins last night."

Marsh eyed this quiet man, and then clapped him on the back. "Congratulations! Boys, girls, what are their names?"

Beneath the beard he felt his face redden. "Names? Uh, undecided. They're boys."

"Well, that's just fine! Now what do you need here? You better load up and get back up the road. Those boys need names."

Thomas followed Marsh's advice. The hundred pound bag of flour, the small keg of nails and a can of talc that Marsh recommended were tucked in the back near the dirty baby bed. He headed out of town knowing that news of the births would spread throughout the valley as farmers and miners stopped by the general store.

\* \* \*

Back at the ranch, Mom Manwaring came into the bedroom with a cup of tea to greet a very tired Sarah Ann. Mom had been present at Lincoln's delivery. Lincoln, a husky little guy, had greeted the world on his own terms. Sarah Ann's own mother had been present for the birth of her first son, John James Manwaring, and her dainty daughter, Amy. Sarah Ann knew she birthed babies well and that twins were a double blessing, but her insides were begging for a few days of recovery. As the two women sipped their tea, each was silently considering the sweeping changes she had experienced over the past year.

Mom Manwaring broke the silence. "Thomas drove off early to borrow the Fosters' extra baby bed. I expect he'll head on in to town for flour and to spread the word about these little boys." Sarah Ann listened and agreed, but she knew Thomas was no news spreader. He'd probably tell Marsh and then hightail it back home. Sarah Ann knew her husband's nature. Quiet, self-contained, strong in character, proud and responsible, determined to provide well for his family. This man whom any self-respecting woman could love. The man whom Sarah Ann loved. He understood her stoic manner, which others considered aloof. They matched up well and were now glued together with twins.

"Sarah Ann, what are you going to name these boys?" asked Mom Manwaring.

"Oh, names? I don't even know. When Thomas gets back we'll talk it over. J.J. already owns the grandfathers' names. I've read a lot of names in books. We'll come up with something original. It's not every day a family has twins."

"I think I hear those unnamed boys."

"Oh, dear. Bring them over. Let's see if I can bring up milk for two."

"I'll check on the children. They don't understand 'be quiet' when they are told!" fussed Mom Manwaring, their grandmother.

Sarah Ann gritted her teeth and nursed the twins, determined to soon be out of bed and relieve their grandmother of her duties around the house and her opportunity to criticize, as she believed no one could do things as well as her missing son, the one the Indians took from her.

\* \* \*

The baby boys cried, slept, ate, and received their names, Lester and Leland. The family soon shortened the names to Les and Lee and always talked about them as one. "Les and Lee did this or that," never one of them alone. Sarah Ann took turns using the cradle for one and the little bed for the other until

Thomas finished the second cradle. The bedroom sported wall-to-wall beds with room for Sarah Ann, Thomas, Les, and Lee. The other children, J.J., Amy, and Lincoln, filled the two upstairs bedrooms. The house overflowed with people and the chores never seemed to get completed, until after Christmas when Thomas firmly decided on a working routine.

Thomas, the first person out of bed each morning, stoked the fires to warm the house and heat the range for cooking. He then headed to the barn to milk the big Holstein cow. Amy heated water for the mush to be cooked for breakfast, was responsible for seeing that Lincoln was properly dressed for the day, and saw that the upstairs beds were made. J.J. was responsible for emptying the chamber pots and pumping fresh water for the day's cooking and washing. The working routine allowed time for necessary chores in the house and time for Thomas and J.J. to pitch hay to the cattle for their winter feed.

# A SCHOOLHOUSE
# MARCH 1871

"**SARAH ANN,** the spring work is more than the boy and I can do, even with Lem coming out to help once in a while. I was thinking maybe Lem could move into the first cabin, sort of set it up as a bunkhouse. Room and board could be part of his pay. When the work slows down after harvest, he would be here to help build a schoolhouse."

"He'll eat us out of house and home, but it would be a solution. Remember, that spit bucket for his chaw stays out of my sight!" Sarah Ann laid the ground rules. Lem Stone, Will's younger brother, was also a chewer of plug tobacco.

"Yes, Ma'am," Thomas replied. Plans for the future of the ranch and his family began filling his head. By September he and Lem would be back at the carpentry work they enjoyed doing.

Thomas ordered lumber from the mill to go with the timbers he and Lem had dragged from the mountain. The timbers were well dried and ready for the saw. Thomas made four trips with the hay wagon to bring the lumber from the mill to the site chosen for the school.

The corner where the lane left the main river road seemed right. It was just over a quarter of a mile from the house, close enough for his children to walk. Up Jeff Davis Creek was another homestead as well as up the river. Ranchers and farmers were raising families along with their crops. "No doubt this is the best location for a school," commented Thomas.

"Agreed. Let's get at it," responded Lem. "Seems like we should fence off the schoolyard first, keep the cows out from the pasture side and show where the lane goes so folks will stop cutting the corner when they cross the creek and drive across the site."

Thomas sighed but agreed with Lem. First they would build the fence. Then they would stack the timbers and the lumber from the mill so he and Lem could get right to the building without a lot of extra sawing. They dug a decent foundation and managed to raise the corner timbers without extra help. Framed out and sturdy, the finish work could be done in the winter after the bad weather would drive the men indoors. Behind the main room they would create a back room where a teacher could stay overnight and do a little cooking if he chose. Teachers usually boarded with the family of one of their students, but some private space was practically a necessity, according to Thomas.

"Thomas, where are you planning to put the outhouse?" asked Lem.

"Over in the back on the east side."

"That would be out of sight," observed Lem.

"That's the point. Some privacy," countered Thomas.

"Well, do you have any idea what goes on in the outhouse besides what's supposed to?"

"What?"

"Well, smoking for one. Bullying and fighting for another. Kids do bad stuff when they are out of the teacher's sight and the reach of his switch." Lem sounded as if he knew what he was talking about.

"Where do you think we should put it?" asked Thomas.

Lem scratched his head as he pushed back his sweaty brown hat and perused the site. "I lean toward the southwest corner. Far enough away from the schoolhouse, and the wind will send any odors into the pasture instead of the schoolyard. Best of all, it's in the line of sight from the main door so the teacher could keep track of any unruly activities by standing on the porch during recess time."

Thomas could tell Lem had thought this through. It seemed a good plan, so they put their backs to the task of digging a good deep hole. Sarah Ann would wonder about the hearty appetites they brought to the dinner table, but the outhouse discussion was not appropriate conversation for mealtime in this pioneer home.

At the same time Thomas made plans for the Martin School, the Dearborns up the river were building a school for their children and neighbors. The prolific families of the upper valley had enough children for two one-room schools, about ten miles apart. It made sense for both families to appeal to the Oregon State Board of Education for charters to operate their schools. John Dearborn and Thomas rode to Baker City and located an educated man named Nelson who agreed to live with the Dearborns for six months while teaching at their Marysville School and then moving to the Martins for the next six months to teach at their school. Education for the handful of children near the Martin place was about to begin.

# JANUARY 1872

**AMY AND LINCOLN** went eagerly up the lane to school. J.J. pursued his education under duress from Sarah Ann and Thomas. He referred to Thomas as Pa, but he kept his own last name of Manwaring. He was the only child who kept a treasured memory of his natural father. He imagined a heroic person who fought Indians, adventured to the west and back, and tried to bring his family to an exciting life in Oregon. Sarah Ann did little to correct his dreams. J.J.'s grandmother, Mom Manwaring, enhanced the memories with her own recollections of her son.

Amy loved school. The Damon girls became her friends. Books became her friends, also. Sarah Ann could see her relating to the stories, the romance of literature even as a nine-year-old. She treasured her time at school recess when she could giggle with the other girls. What a break from the house of brothers and a mother whose mouth knew no upturned corners and whose eyes were grey like the sky on a cloudy day. Amy walked to school with her younger brother Lincoln, who was in first grade. First graders always like school and Lincoln was no exception.

The Martin School set a goal of educating children through grade eight. For the most part, that covered reading, writing, numbers, and the history of the country. Talk of the Civil War provided history and a basis for current events. The first settlers in the area had been a group of miners who found gold up Dixie Creek, so named because they were Southern sympathizers. Feelings still ran high on the topic. Prejudice dies hard and the children in school knew it. As time passed, some settlers were embarrassed to admit to fighting for the Confederacy.

# OCTOBER 1872

**GEORGE CAME** into the world with little fanfare in October of 1872. This stocky baby with a healthy yowl replaced the twins as the infant of the family. Sarah Ann picked his name,

George Thomas. He could not be named after either of his grandfathers because J.J. held both John and James as names. When he opened his eyes, folks remarked how grey they were, just like Sarah Ann's. He nursed like a boy, nothing dainty about him. As he grew, walked and talked, he found numerous ways to gain attention. His life seemed to be spent trying to keep up with Les and Lee. It hardly seemed fair that they were a pair with long legs and he was the stubby chaser in all games. Sometimes Lincoln took pity and joined his team against the others to make things fair. George became Link's little buddy. When he outgrew the baby bed, he crawled in with Lincoln for a good night's sleep. Sarah Ann and Thomas were glad for the peace and let the bigger upstairs room be the boys' dormitory. J.J. moved to the porch for privacy. Thomas closed it in for winter to keep out the cold.

* * *

Thomas and Lem worked well together. With two men on the place, the ranch became more productive. A few more cattle filled the fields, more calves were born, and there were more steers to sell. The profit always returned to the land to improve it or purchase more. Lem helped with the apple orchard that Thomas and Will, Lem's brother, had planted in the beginning when they were just a couple of knock-around bachelors who had tired of mining. Thomas, with a serious bent to his personality, provided the "straight man" for Lem, the prankster. Both of them were good-natured and managed to avoid serious trouble by just being smart and cagey. The orchard stood for a successful venture. The trees matured enough to provide all the apples the family could use as well as boxes to take to town to sell in front of Marsh's store.

"Hey, Thomas, get those kids out here to help pick these apples," quipped Lem. The kids thought apple picking was fun in the beginning. First they picked the pale green Transparents, Sarah Ann's favorite for applesauce, followed by the Jonathans, the best eating apple ever created. Later in the season the treasured Gravensteins were harvested for pies.

"Ma, make us an apple pie," begged Lincoln. It took at least two pies for supper. Sarah Ann never minded because her pies were special, with flaky crusts made with lard and flour, and apples sweetened just right and spiced up with cinnamon.

She knew Lem had whispered to Lincoln, "Go ask your ma to make us some pie." After supper Lem managed to carry a piece out to the log cabin that had become his personal bunkhouse. Sarah Ann felt flattered that Lem craved her pies. Apple season ended when the crab apples filled the last box. They were tiny to pick, and the children lost interest in the task, but the crab apple jelly made from them turned morning biscuits into everyone's favorite treat.

The money made from apple sales was designated for something special, a trip to Canyon City to the county seat, a hike to Strawberry Lake for some high country fishing, or maybe an overnight to Baker City to shop for new material for shirts and dresses. Not all ranchers were as frugal as the Martins, who saved up for special outings that were worth remembering. Sarah Ann saw that everyone was properly dressed and ready to practice good manners if they went to a restaurant, like the Blue Cup Café in Baker City or the Trowbridge Hotel in John Day. A woman from New York held certain standards for her family. Thanks to Lem who stayed home and took care of the ranch, Sarah Ann could occasionally engineer an apple money escape.

When the circuit rider came for church services, most families came to town to hear the "good news" and share in a potluck dinner at noon. Most folks looked forward to this event every couple of months. Many were eagerly waiting for the Idaho diocese to extend to Eastern Oregon as the preachers from the Willamette Valley found the trip over the Cascades or up the Columbia River too daunting. Except for Mr. Larson, who followed the *Truth Seekers Around the World*, the Prairie City farmers and businessmen held typical Victorian views of life and behavior. Even Lem joined the family for church and the neighborly visits after. The good food at the potluck dinner drew him there as well.

# APRIL 1873

**WHEN THOMAS MARTIN** left Missouri in 1859, he headed for the gold fields of California. Partially successful, he earned enough to migrate north to the Willamette Valley of Western Oregon. As a single man, he only toyed with the idea of homesteading there. "Get rich quick," urged the other single men he met, who encouraged him to head for mining in Idaho.

After a season of Idaho mining, Thomas said to himself, "This hard work is not providing me a permanent lifestyle." Then he repeated it to his friends, Will and Matt. They agreed it was time to move on, so the men joined together to homestead in the John Day Valley.

Thomas had left his mother and his younger siblings in Missouri. Herman, Thomas's younger brother, chose to come in 1873. He arrived in Prairie City without forewarning. The best to do for him was to share the little log house with Lem. He helped on the ranch, but as families go, he was not eager to do as his older brother expected. He enjoyed a drink on occasion, which Sarah Ann and Thomas did not cotton to. If Lem joined him for the drink, there were two workers not worth their salt the next day. Herman was asked to move on.

Thomas had thought long and hard about what he would say to his brother. He settled on, "I have a family to raise and a ranch to tend. Your presence is an interference. I took care of you when we lived in Missouri, but you're a grown man now. It's time for you to take care of yourself." When he delivered the speech, Herman packed up and rode off to town on his pinto horse without even a wave good-bye.

# SEPTEMBER 1874

**CLASSES BEGAN** in the fall of '74 at the Martin School. Mr. Nelson agreed to teach from September 1 until February 1 when he would move up to the Marysville School. Two boys a year younger than J.J. entered school. Their family had homesteaded a second place up Jeff Davis Creek. The boys, Fred and Hector, were cousins, and from day one they gave J.J. a bad time. They teased him because he had to walk his little sister and brother to school. Both boys were good readers who made fun of J.J.'s stammering over the difficult words. Mr. Nelson's teaching technique included a startling whack on the desk with a ruler when answers were wrong. At recess when the students were released to go to the outhouse, they would barge in before J.J. was finished. The worst was when Fred said, "Hey, J.J., I saw your mother the other day. It must be true about your dad."

"What are you talking about?" asked J.J.

"She is pretty crabby looking. I heard your dad didn't get killed by Indians. He just decided to ride over the hill to get away from your ugly mom," teased Hector.

"You take that back!" shouted J.J. as he took a swing at Hector's jaw. Mr. Nelson arrived out the schoolhouse door just in time to grab J.J. by the collar and escort him to the corner of the classroom where he had to sit and listen to the snickers from his classmates. The whacks administered after school did not compare to the distress at hearing the hateful remarks about his mother and his hero, his missing father.

Sarah Ann and Thomas were not happy about the fighting at school. On the way home, J.J. had threatened Amy and Link with big trouble if they told what had happened. He would not share the reason for the fight with his parents, so he earned an extra round of chores at home to help him remember to keep his temper. One of those chores was to empty the chamber pots into the big bucket with the flip-up lid and dispose of the contents in the outhouse. He always took his turn at the job, but now it was solely his job every day for the next two weeks.

Fred's and Hector's parents were luckless farmers and soon gave up their homestead and moved on. J.J. was glad to see them go and so was Thomas because he was able to buy the property and increase the size of the ranch with land that shared its border. The acquisition required more work. Thomas and Lem split rails to build fences. Then they rode to Vale to get some more cattle. They drove them home over the Dixie Mountain pass, a fine new Hereford bull and four good-looking cows. They kept the bull in the barn until the rail fence was finished and he could be turned into the pasture with the rest of the herd. Thomas anticipated some fine calves in the spring.

# LITTLE MARY'S FAMILY
# MARCH 1875

**BABY MARY WAS BORN.** The whole family seemed enamored with her. Finally a baby girl had joined the household of brothers. Amy loved caring for her. It was like having a live doll. Mary's disposition matched her curls and dimples. Sarah Ann treasured the quiet time spent nursing her. She would contemplate her family, wishing she could understand the boys, especially J.J., who shared his discontent too freely for her liking. In fact, she heard his boots clumping up the back steps one day as he came home from school. Being in a growly mood, he stayed outside, thinking about his unhappiness with life.

Sarah Ann could hear J.J. talking to himself from the back steps. "I call Thomas Martin 'Pa,' but my name is still Manwaring. As I see it, life is just not fair." Recurring thoughts took over his mind.

"The twins were born. Was that ever a ton of work! My share of chores grew more numerous and more difficult. No one seemed to appreciate my work. In fact they kept talking about how I needed to go to school, improve my reading and such. I used to read with Ma, sitting on her lap. When I got too big for that, I would pull up a chair beside her. But her lap filled up with baby brothers, and reading went by the wayside.

"George, the next brother, was born in '72. That was the year Pa built a schoolhouse. It sat up the lane about half a mile from our house. The neighbors who lived up river and up Jeff Davis Creek sent their children to school whenever a teacher could be found. I am older than quite a few of the students, but I can't read much better. Truth be told, I hate school. I'm always first out the schoolhouse door, leaving Amy and Lincoln to walk home together to this house where all the little kids and babies live. I'll hurry into the kitchen and try to get out before Ma asks me to watch the twins and George. Les and Lee aren't too bad, but stumpy little George has a mind of his own and is no fun to keep track of.

"As soon as Amy gets home I'll go to the barn, saddle up my horse, Little Brown, and head over to Grandpa Manwaring's. Mom Manwaring will have fresh cookies and time to talk to me. Grandpa will tell me how I remind him of his son, my real dad. The Manwaring spread is a great place for me. It's not as large as Pa Martin's. Grandpa is not trying to get more land all the time. He doesn't push me to 'get an education' the way Ma and Pa do."

# THE BOYS

**AMY AND LINCOLN APPEARED** on the steps, home from school. Lincoln and the little boys ran out under the big fir that canopied their special play area, a miniature fort and a pretend flourmill with Indians coming around the bend behind the trunk. The battle began. Lincoln and George held the fort. Les and Lee arrived with war whoops. The battle ended as the settlers (Lincoln and George) who had gathered to save the mill, lie exhausted in their safety. The two braves tore on by, not stopping to harass the settlers or burn the fort. The boys imagined the soldiers from Fort Logan coming into sight, scaring the Indians into the mountains as they headed toward the Wallowas. Lincoln had heard the story so often he thought he would puke if he heard it again, how the Prairie City town people saved the flourmill when unfriendly Indians danced about in the hills.

# AMY

**AMY TIPTOED BY** Sarah Ann to peek at Mary. She took a seat on the stairs to look at her ma and the baby. She thought, *Finally, I have a sister. Imagine! She will grow up to be my playmate, but now she is a baby . . . like having a big new doll. Ma will put her in the cradle so I can rock her to sleep. Her little round face is surrounded by wispy curls. Her lips make a smile, like Pa Martin. The little boys have straight mouths like my mother. Unless they are laughing, they all look a little grim. My mother and my real father were cousins, but only my ma got the straight mouth. The picture of my father makes him look like a gentle adventurer with a mustache. I guess men are proud to grow whiskers, mustaches to look manly and beards to keep their faces and necks warm in winter. Uh oh, I must have been ruminating about stuff. Ma just called me to do my kitchen chores.*

Amy's green dress swished around the kitchen as she located the silverware and plates and put them at their proper places at the table. The lace on the cuff of her dress got wet and dirty as she scrubbed the potatoes. "*I should have rolled up the sleeves,*" she thought." *Now my lace cuffs will be dirty when I go to school tomorrow. I just love lace. I am the only girl at school who has lace on her everyday dress. Ma makes me feel special with the dresses she makes for me. I think she has a proper sense of style because she came from New York.*

"Amy, call the boys to wash-up for supper," repeated Ma.

*Oh my, ruminating again. "Ruminate" is the new word I learned in school today. Look at the dirt on those boys, especially on George. I'll have to scrub him up at the back porch. I'll get some water from the pump, heat it up a bit on the kitchen stove, and pop George's hands and face into the sink. The sink has a drain hole that carries the used water out to the yard. The weeds and grass are always green where the water goes. His stubby fingers and round face will sparkle when I get through with him. He'll be the cleanest boy at the supper table.*" Amy looked up as she heard J.J. riding into the corral.

He was talking to himself. "Here I come on sweaty Little Brown. I galloped him all the way home to get here in time for my chores. Too late. Pa will know the horse has been on a run without permission. I wish he would yell at me. Instead he will carry that disappointed look on his face and bless me with the silent treatment. I think he wishes I were not here. So why is there so much disapproval when I ride off? He just wants me to do work. I am hoping to avoid a conversation concerning my whereabouts after school today."

Thomas roosted at the head of the table where he said the evening blessing. Supper was rather quiet with a sense of anticipation in the air. The family cleared their plates. Thomas put water on to heat so Sarah Ann and Amy could do the dishes. Then he said, "J.J., meet me on the porch please." Thomas did not expect an argument, so J.J. slid across the homemade bench and got another sliver in his butt. He examined a hairy spider on the edge of the sink, anything to keep from looking at Thomas, who sat down beside him with his elbows on his knees. J.J. could smell the work odor of Thomas's day mixed with the barnyard dung that blew toward the porch. "J.J., I think you are old enough to hear some things I've never shared with you," he began.

"I was born in Kentucky. When the 1840 Census taker came by our place, he recorded our ages, whether we were boys or girls and if we could read or not. I was eight years old and I had two little sisters and a baby brother. My mother and father were in their thirties. Mother could read pretty well, but my father was not so good. Not long after the Census taker had called on us, we packed up and headed for Missouri Territory. My father took sick while we were there and finally died. Mother was hard-pressed to take care of my sisters, a baby brother and me. She did laundry for people and I found various odd jobs to get some money. No matter how we got along, Mother made me read and get what education I could. She would say, 'If your father had only had an education he would have survived in Missouri instead of dying from the hard work he was forced to do.'

"I took her words seriously and did become educated. I helped her with the family until the wanderlust yanked so hard, I just had to get going. By then the rest of the family could do their part to take care of themselves. That's when I headed for California, rode on up to the Willamette Valley, and finally landed here in eastern Oregon. Now I have a wonderful life with your ma and I love all you children. But I'm telling you my story because I understand how it is to be a young boy with the weight of responsibility for the family when a father dies. My father was my hero just like your father was to you. That's how boys think on their fathers. One man used to call on my mother, but I could not cotton up to him. He was not my father and I wouldn't give him a chance to be a substitute. I was afraid he would try to tell me what to do.

"Maybe you feel like I did. I can understand if you do. But it would not be good for you or the rest of this family if you set the wrong example of not minding what I say and not doing your best to become educated. We are not going out to the woodshed this evening where the strap is hanging. It is there to encourage rebellious boys to do what is expected of them. You think about what I have shared with you and let me know tomorrow if you see things my way or if just taking the strapping would be a better way to learn."

Thomas got up slowly from their shared bench and ambled into the kitchen, leaving J.J. to his thinking.

Thomas watched Sarah Ann rocking Mary. His talk with J.J. had put him in a contemplative mood. He thought, *I am a God-fearing, honest man. The residents of the John Day Valley who know me respect me as such. I contribute to the Methodist Church Fund that is collected to pay the circuit preacher who comes every few months. Sarah Ann and I wash up the kids and take them all to meeting when a Sunday service is held. Marsh Howard has some land he will donate for a church when we get ready to build one. I've seen some plans the diocese sent over for a church with a steeple and a place for a good loud bell. I pay my bills and feed my family. I built a school for my children and the neighbors' young ones who live up the river and on Jeff Davis Creek. To homestead and buy land fascinates me. Unlike my pa, I will one day have land for my offspring to ranch and farm.*

\* \* \*

George was jealous of Mary, who took his ma's attention away. He couldn't come crying when the boys gave him a bad time. It looked as if he would like to yank Mary's baby curls to make her cry, a way of saying, "Look at me!" No mother would stand for that so he'd be in big trouble, sitting in his high chair facing the corner of the kitchen until he was forgiven. George was just one more cog in the overflowing wheel of this family.

"Ma, come quick! George cut his head!" Amy announced. George ran around on two-year-old legs trying to copy the antics of his brothers. This time he had tripped and cut his chin on the boot scraper Thomas had created from a broken shovel blade attached to the back step. Sarah Ann handed baby Mary to Amy to hold as she tended to George. She washed his chin with soap and water and treated it with a dab of alcohol which brought more wails from the little boy, so a hug was in order with a piece of clean cloth and some tape. A quiet George did not want to give up his mother's lap. Just like his older siblings, he learned that a new baby took precedence on her lap, which was ample, but only big enough for one. George learned it, but he did not like it.

Peeking around the corner, the twins invited him to come out to play "Fort Logan," and he slipped off Sarah Ann's lap and headed toward the back door. Everyone in the family remembered the recent Indian scare. Renegades spotted on the ridge prompted farmers to wagon-up their families and head for the flourmill where sacks could be piled up for protection. The false alarm lasted a day. Ranchers headed home to tend their stock. Sarah Ann's letter to her mother about the excitement no doubt worried the New York relatives about her safety in the far West. Fort Logan no longer housed the detachment of soldiers who had once protected the valley. Heavy walls built with foot wide logs still stood around the perimeter of a fort that could be returned to active duty if necessary, but every year the fort deteriorated, leaving valley residents in charge of their own safety. Indians were not the prime concern. By 1874 building warm houses, surviving long winters and short hot summers, growing food to feed families, and earning money to buy necessities kept everyone hard at work.

* * *

One of those necessities arrived at the Martin ranch after Thomas had taken cattle to Baker City to sell. A new cook stove weighed down the bed of the wagon. Thomas and Lem wiggled it through the kitchen door and wedged it against the east wall. They attached the existing stovepipe, and then decided a new pipe was needed for safety. After a trip to Marsh's to get it, the stove finally stood proudly in the kitchen. How grand the warming ovens on top appeared to Sarah Ann. Food could stay warm while something else baked or roasted in the oven. The left-hand side housed the firebox and behind it a hot water well to provide warm water for washing dishes at the end of a meal and for washing hands and faces in the morning. The water stayed warm even after the fire went out. Yes, 1875 brought Sarah Ann her darling baby girl and her fancy new stove.

She could bake three apple pies at once in the new oven. Apples stored in the cellar magically appeared on the kitchen counter every time Lem came from the cellar. He went for potatoes or squash but always returned with apples, also. Sarah Ann made pie or cobbler so often she feared a shortage of sugar from her hundred pound sack. Apples won't keep all winter, so the baking frenzy came to an end. It would begin again in the summer when berries became available. The family favorite, huckleberries, resulted in at least one or two outings. Every child was responsible for a tin can with a string bail that had been fashioned by making a nail hole on either side and slipping the string through. The little kids, even George, carried a bucket made from a tin. J.J. and Amy carried larger buckets because they could be trusted not to trip on branches in the woods and spill all their berries. They could also be trusted not to eat more than the allotted handful of the treasured berries. All waited for the end of the day when they could gobble huckleberry pie for supper's dessert.

When the oven needed cleaning, J.J. was again called into service. It seemed to him that his chores encompassed women's as well as men's work. "Fourteen is an unfair age," he grumbled, "no two ways about it!" Sarah Ann studied her fuming fourteen-year-old from across the room. In her opinion he needed to learn some things: the value of work, the value of an education, the value of controlling one's temper. She counted on Thomas to do his job instilling these values.

Amy surpassed J.J. as far as schoolwork went. She read for pleasure, creeping upstairs with a romantic tale whenever she was not summoned for chores or watching the boys. If the task included playing with the baby, it was a different story. Darling, dimpled Mary was the live doll Amy dreamed of. Cooing and laughing, she rarely cried. Sarah Ann dressed her in the pretty little dresses she had been dreaming of making every time another boy entered the family.

Sarah Ann taught Amy to sew, more than just mending and replacing buttons. Amy laid out a pattern on the kitchen table, pinned it to fabric and very carefully cut around the pattern. She hand-basted the pieces together and sewed them on Sarah Ann's treadle machine. "Watch those stitches closely or you'll be ripping it out to make it right," cautioned Sarah Ann. All the time Amy pushed the treadle without stopping, forward toes, backward heels, over and over. She first made a blue chambray pinafore for Mary to wear over her dress to keep it clean. It served as a giant bib. Proud of her work, Amy vowed she would do even better so she could dress Mary as well as her ma had dressed her. The romance novels she read filled her dream world of cooking and sewing for a husband and her own family one day. Amy was the age to continue her dreams through books and writing in the velvet journal she received at Christmas.

# CHRISTMAS 1875

*Dear Diary,*

*You are my first store bought gift. I love the softness of your red velvet cover and the fancy silver letters on the front. Today is Christmas. We are taking some special time away from chores to celebrate. Pa and Ma look at celebrating Christmas differently because they came from different circumstances as children. Ma will tell us about her holiday celebration when she was a child in New York. I must hurry downstairs to hear her story once again.*

*Amy*

**SARAH ANN BEGAN** when she saw Amy enter the room. "I remember coach lights lit on the corners and decorations in all the neighbors' houses in our neighborhood. My family cooked their own holiday dinner at home—a large piece of meat, vegetables from the cellar, pies from the oven, accompanied by breads with sweet cream butter and jam from the blackberry patch. The dinner was special and complete when guests arrived to share it. Fragrant greens decorated the dining area. After eating, the Christmas story filled the air as each child took her turn reading. We each received a gift, usually homemade, and when the fire died down, carried it off to bed."

Thomas said, "Let me tell you about Christmas when my family lived in Missouri. Winters were cold. We walked to church in our everyday clothes, which were not warm enough. My mother, brother, sisters and I shared a meal at the church with other hardworking families. When we got home, Mother would read the Christmas story again, then she sent us all to bed where she had tucked a piece of fruit and a sweet treat under each pillow. Those gifts were dear and greatly appreciated by us children."

The Martins celebrated Christmas on the ranch by taking time to share the story read from Thomas's well-worn Bible. Cooking a holiday meal resembled nearly every other day of meal preparation. Just as many people came to eat, just as much food filled each plate as every ordinary day, but no one went back to work after the noon dinner. "Everyone should help clean up the kitchen," said Amy, and they did.

Sarah Ann had cooked the wild turkey Lem had shot. It was no easy job to clean out the buckshot and make it tender. She roasted it "long and slow," and covered it with a heavy lid after brining it overnight. The salty meat shared its flavor with a large pot of potatoes. Lem and Lincoln brought them in from the cellar after de-sprouting the whole bin so they would last another few months. Thomas contributed one of the hams from the smokehouse. Two kinds of meat would stretch a week's supply of food and Sarah Ann, the cook, could take a breather from all the preparations.

One extra guest came to the Christmas table: Thomas's brother, Uncle Herman. He and Thomas got along fine now that Herman lived in town on his own. They reminisced about the hard times in Missouri after their father died. Herman, the youngest of Thomas's family, couldn't even remember that the Martin family had once lived in Campbell County, Tennessee.

No vacation from ranch work came during a holiday week. Every morning the two new Jersey cows were milked and relieved of their full bags of cream-rich liquid. Their output surpassed the one old Holstein Thomas sold to the neighbors. The pails filled the bottom shelf of the icebox. As it cooled, the milk sank to the bottom of the pail and the cream rose to the top. Sarah Ann scooped it off and saved it until there was enough to make butter. The older children took their turns at churning until butter appeared. The buttermilk left over improved Sarah Ann's biscuit batter and Lem even liked to drink it.

One blessing of winter was the ease with which things could be kept cool. In summer they depended on the supply of ice in the icehouse, chunks of it cut from the frozen banks of the John Day River and packed in sawdust gleaned from the lumbering activities that furthered the many building projects Thomas envisioned for the ranch.

After the holiday, Thomas began thinking about his mother. She was now an old lady still living in Missouri with his sister, Charity. "Sarah Ann, what would you think of having my mother come west for a visit? It would cost something, but it would be good to see her again."

"Would she stay with us?"

"I thought she could share Amy's room."

"Just like a man," thought Sarah Ann, but she knew Thomas needed to see his mother if possible. She sensed there was unfinished business between them, and that her kind, tolerant husband craved the chance to unburden himself, to explain why he left Missouri and the family that had depended on him from the time he was a young boy.

"She would be good help with the children and the cooking. My mother is not lazy," said Thomas.

Sarah Ann gave a bit of a smile. Behind it was the thought that another woman in the kitchen might not be as welcome as her husband seemed to think. "Why don't you write her and see what kind of reply you get. See if she feels up to making such a trip."

Thomas agreed and put himself to the task with a pen, ink, and some of Sarah Ann's fine writing paper saved for special correspondence.

\* \* \*

Mail that came on the weekly stage in the middle of April included a detailed letter from Pa's mother, Mary Martin. He opened and read it at the supper table so everyone could hear the news.

> *Dear Tommy,*
>
> *I have read and reread your kind invitation to come to Prairie City for a visit. Getting to know Sarah Ann and the children has been a dream of mine that I thought could never be fulfilled. Herman has also been gone from home a long time and I would like to see him. If I leave my work at the Empire Hotel, the position will not be available upon my return. Charity could make the trip with me. I think it would be a safer trip with two women travelling together rather than one alone. Herman is willing and eager to get a larger place for Charity to share with him. You said I could share Amy's room at your house. I promise to be no trouble to her and please thank her for me.*

> *With this in mind, I feel that if I make the trip, it would be a permanent move as there is nothing in Missouri for me to come back to. I appreciate your kind offer and await an answer so travel plans may be made.*
>
> *My love to you all,*
>
> *Mother Martin*

Sarah Ann studied Pa's expression behind his beard. She wondered if the part about the permanent visit had registered with him as it had with her. The children waited for their parents to respond, but an uncomfortable pause filled the kitchen. Mary cooed from her high chair; George wondered why everyone was quiet. "So Grandmother Martin is coming for a visit?" asked Lincoln.

"Oh, good!" exclaimed Les and Lee together, a two-boy chorus as usual.

"Gram Matter?" asked three-year-old George.

"Well, Grandmother Mary Martin is my mother. I haven't seen her for many years, over 15 in fact. She wants to get to know my family; that's all of you. It has been far too long." Sarah Ann saw a tear in his eye, sentimental man that he was.

Amy put the punctuation to the conversation. "She wants to move in with us. I expect I'll get to know her best of all when she moves into my room."

Amy had anticipated that she would soon be sharing her room, but thought it would be with little Mary, the darling baby, not Pa's mother, an old woman she didn't even know. She had never even seen a picture of her. Sarah Ann could see some ruffled feathers would have to be smoothed.

"I think early fall would be the best time for her trip," said Sarah Ann.

J.J. had no comment. He had one grandmother he knew, Mom Manwaring, and not much interest in getting to know another. The table was cleared. Dishes found their homes on the various shelves. Soon the little boys were tucked in their beds. Les and Lee shared the full-sized bed, George slept in a smaller ¾ bed and Lincoln had the other full one all to himself. If George woke up during the night, he crawled in with Link, who was a hard sleeper and didn't care. Amy came to her mother's room before she went to bed. "Do I have to share with Grandmother Martin? My room is the smallest. What will we do when Mary stops nursing and needs her own room? How old is Pa's mother? Do you think she will live very long? I bet she snores."

"Amy, enough! Pa will figure it out. He may make a new bed. She won't get here for a few months. We have time to get used to the idea and think about it positively. Pa wants to care for his mother. That part of his nature is the same quality that makes him care for all of us. He is a man who ponders things before he acts. Let's give him time to work everything out. Lord knows, we can use an extra hand with cooking and mending. She is in her sixties. Lots of people work hard in their sixties. They don't need to be coddled and cared for, and I'm sure she won't either. Now I expect you to be a gracious young lady about the whole thing. That's the way I brought you up."

Amy cried that night in bed, but never anywhere else. Grandmother Martin did not fit into her dreams.

Sarah Ann lay in bed, still awake after Amy went upstairs. "Pa, do you think Herman will really find a place for your sister Charity? That is an important part of this whole arrangement. We simply cannot house two extra women permanently. What if we have another baby? You take your responsibilities very seriously and never let things interfere with your family's well-being," Sarah Ann reminded.

"Sarah, don't press me. I need time to think things over and figure it out. I'll let you read my reply letter to Mother when I get it ready to be sure we are in agreement."

Sarah Ann rolled her eyes, but not where her husband could see. She turned away from the light and let Thomas turn down the wick so they could go to sleep.

# J.J. BECOMES A MAN
## APRIL 1876

**"NO ONE IS HAPPIER** than I am," thought J.J. "The school year is over! My eighth grade education is complete. The teacher thinks I should come back for one more year. He says I need to improve my math skills. He keeps preaching that every man needs to be able to count his money, earn it, save it, and invest it in something. If I had any money, I could count it just fine. I'm wiry and strong and I should be paid for my work. I have made up my mind!"

His parents' desire for him to get more education fell on deaf ears. Thomas finally sighed and said, "I think J.J. needs to experience life away from the ranch for a summer. He won't freeze, as the weather is good. Mom Manwaring will feed him whenever he shows up at their place. We will keep his bed available in the back porch room. I may have to hire another hand to help Lem and me get the hay up, but this will be the best for the boy."

Sarah Ann thought he was too young, but she was weary of his willfulness and complaints about Thomas. She longed for some peace. Many boys quit school after eighth grade. It looked as if J.J. would be one of them. Sarah Ann knew she would hear criticism from Mom Manwaring when she found out that her grandson was loose on his own. She would not be surprised to see him go to his grandparents and ask to stay. He could be a big help to Captain Manwaring, who was aging and having trouble doing all his work. But was J.J. the "man" for the job? Sarah Ann doubted it. He had been taught how to do things, but no one could teach him to have the will to do what he had been taught. Joy in a job well done—not part of his make-up.

**"J.J., GO AHEAD** and look for work somewhere else for the summer. Your bed is here and always available," said Thomas.

Sarah Ann had figured it correctly. J.J. headed for the Manwarings' first thing when Thomas said, "OK, and your bed is always available. Come on back anytime you feel like helping out here." Thomas was a wise man about kids, letting them run with it when they felt the need for independence. Sarah Ann held a mother's fear for her offspring. Consequently, she prayed for the power to control, that is everyone except her husband. He was the quiet-mannered "boss" of their home.

\* \* \*

"Why, John James, what are you doing here?" asked Mom Manwaring as she heard his footsteps on her porch. Little Brown was tied to the fence. Mom Manwaring noticed a good-sized backpack tied behind the saddle. "You look like a traveling man."

"Pa said I could come to town and look for work. I figured your place is closer to town. Could I stay with you?"

"Sure, honey, anytime . . . Oh, you mean live here?" Mom Manwaring clarified.

"Well, if you wouldn't mind. I could help the captain with his work, and I sure do like your cooking, Mom Manwaring."

*And he looks and talks like my Cody boy,* thought Mom Manwaring as she tried to ignore the catch in her throat. "Let's talk to the captain about it. I bet he'll like the idea of some help and a man to talk to over the supper table."

J.J. turned Little Brown into the corral and brought his pack as far as the front door. Then he took a seat at Mom Manwaring's kitchen table. Something smelled really good and he knew Captain would soon be in to eat his dinner. The captain's sister was his ma's mother who lived in New York. J.J. always tried to keep it straight in his head. When cousins got married, the confusion of names made it difficult to keep everybody straight. Ma's mother's name was Manwaring before she married James Hunt. J. J. was named John after the captain (whose first name was John) and James Hunt (who was his other grandfather who lived in New York). Ma's name was Hunt before she married J.J.'s father and became a Manwaring. Then she married Pa Martin. She became a Martin, but J.J. remained a Manwaring. He was proud to be a Manwaring. J.J. was glad to see Captain coming up the steps so he could quit thinking about all this name stuff.

"Look who's here," beamed Mom Manwaring.

"I saw his horse in the corral. What brings you here in the middle of the day, J.J.?"

Now J.J. needed to explain it just right. "School is over for the year so I've finished eighth grade. I could go back for another year, but I don't want to do that. Pa says I can work on the ranch because if you're not in school, you need to work. Ma always backs him up. So I thought I might try my hand at working somewhere else. I'm going to look in town for a job, but I wondered if I could stay with you while I do that. I could help you with your work when you needed me, do your chores and such." J.J. stopped for a breath.

Captain leaned back in his chair and studied the boy, just as he would study any man. It was hard to ignore the resemblance to his own boy, Cody. J.J. squirmed a bit in the chair, but tried hard to look the part of a man. "Are you still on good terms with your ma and pa? When a man strikes out on his own he mustn't leave hard feelings behind."

"Well, I know Pa was counting on my help this summer and Ma always wants me to 'go to school, get an education,' but she isn't arguing with Pa and he actually seems to understand my need to get out, I'll say that for him. He said my bed would be there when I decided to come home." J.J. stretched the truth in answer to Captain's question.

"I expect we could give it a try. I just don't want any hard feelings. We're all family; everyone who came in our 'train' is family, bonded as they say."

Captain seemed to forget Thomas Martin, J.J.'s stepdad, did not come in the Manwaring train. He was already here in '69. That's why he was ahead of everybody else in grabbing the land that came available. J.J. thought he should just be content with what they had.

They ate Mom Manwaring's dinner in silence. Chicken, and it wasn't even Sunday! J.J. thought, *So far, so good. I'm going to like it here.*

The captain and Mom Manwaring had a little back room with a cot where J.J. tossed his pack. "Better hang up your clean shirt," prompted Mom Manwaring from the doorway. The doorway, draped with a piece of fabric that hung to the side over a hook, led from the kitchen to this little room that served also as a pantry. Nearly empty shelves lined the west wall. In the fall Mom Manwaring would fill them with the jars in which she had canned her garden produce. The captain would butcher the yearling steer he kept in his south pasture. Maybe this year he would have it parted out at the butcher shop that had recently reopened after the fire. Some meat salted and some meat canned provided food for most of a year.

*That's an idea. I'll check with Butcher Cleaver for a job. I know about meat cutting because we have done it every year at the ranch,* thought J.J.

"Hey, Captain, I think I'll ride down and see if Old Man Cleaver needs some help in his butcher shop."

"That's a good idea, but why don't you give Little Brown a rest? It's only a mile to town; it'll be a nice little walk."

J.J. realized that living with the Manwarings would still put him in a place where grown-ups told one what to do just because they thought they could. He did know how to be respectful, however, and these grandparents did deserve his respect.

Two tracks made up what Captain called a road. It followed Dixie Creek to town. Trees and brush along the creek showed their green buds, promising blossoms. Serviceberries provide white blossoms. A little later mock orange would fill the creek banks with its strong unmistakable fragrance. This pleasant walk took J.J. to his first interview.

"Mr. Cleaver, how are you? I'm J.J. Manwaring, and I'm looking for a job."

"Well, J.J., I don't need any help just now, but check with me later on after my business picks up. We were burned out, you know."

"I did know. I even saw the fire the day it happened. This new building is really fine."

"Some folks think it's too fancy, but I wanted it to say 'butcher shop' to anyone who saw it." Above the front door, a bull head carved from stone guarded the entrance. It matched the rest of the stone front and truly was fancy for this farming town. J.J. agreed it was fancy, but it was in keeping with the business. His disappointment at not getting the first job he tried for showed on his face as he headed down the street.

Glancing to the left down the little side street just past the post office/stage stop, J.J. saw Mrs. Grant sweeping the wood platform where people disembarked from the stage. "Howdy there, Mrs. Grant."

She looked up from the task to see a slender but wiry boy. He looked strong enough, for someone his age. She guessed him to be about 14. "Hello, young man," she replied. "What can I do for you? Expecting mail? It comes on Thursdays."

"I know. I'm not looking for any letters. I'm really looking for work as I am now finished with school. I could do your sweeping for you," J.J. offered.

Mrs. Grant pushed back the escaping wisps of hair from her bun. "I only sweep Saturday and Wednesday, but I could pay you a nickel to do it for me twice a week. This is a busy season for extra time in the garden and spring chores at home."

J.J. gave a smile as he accepted her proposition. "My name is J.J. Manwaring and I live with Captain and Mom Manwaring. They are my grandparents."

Mrs. Grant gave a nod and a bit of a smile herself. She knew the story well, as did nearly everyone in the valley. She also knew J.J.'s Ma and Pa Martin. The postmaster and his wife knew everyone. "I'll see you Saturday. I like it done in the morning, about eight o'clock."

"I'll be here, Mrs. Grant," and he was off through town and up the Dixie Creek road to share the news with Captain.

\* \* \*

J.J. swept the stage platform Saturday morning as promised. Mom Manwaring sent him down the road in plenty of time. Mrs. Grant said he did a fine job and she would have his 5-cent piece ready on Wednesday evening when he completed his first week's work. Mrs. Grant wanted things looking good as people came into town to pick up mail on Saturday, and when the circuit rider came on Sunday she often opened up after the potluck for people to get mail if they had missed Saturday.

\* \* \*

Sarah Ann and Thomas brought the family to church service along with their contribution to the potluck. Sarah Ann went for the mail and Mrs. Grant said, "Your boy J.J. did a fine job sweeping for me yesterday. You've trained him well."

"Thank you," replied Sarah Ann. There seemed nothing else to say. She was not about to share her longing to have the boy back home. Better to let Mrs. Grant think he was out on his own with his parents' blessing. A letter addressed to T.H. Martin from Missouri took her attention from Mrs. Grant. She went to find Thomas and deliver it. The school-age boys were playing tag and tossing balls around. The girls in their best dresses sat on blankets in the park and watched. J.J. was there but didn't take part in the game of tag or throwing balls. After all, he was a working man now.

After church the men held their usual committee meeting about getting a minister and collecting money for a church building. Some of the ladies considered a quilt raffle. The folks from Illinois had some experience with raffles as fundraisers. Maybe the Prairie City residents were well enough established to contribute to a quilt raffle. Some women had some nearly completed quilts, as nearly everyone was always working on a quilt to keep the family beds warm. As one wore out, another was needed to replace it. Sarah Ann was close to finishing a quilt, but if Pa's mother arrived soon it would be needed at the ranch. The letter in her pocket probably held the answer.

\* \* \*

Sarah Ann was just dying to hear the letter, but Thomas was driving the hack and said he'd wait until they got home. Amy sat between her parents, happy to be anywhere else than in the back with the boys. It was better to be holding Mary who had fallen asleep in her arms. She talked to J.J. at the potluck. Mom Manwaring and Captain had no qualms about telling him what to do. She knew this rankled him, but as she saw it, he was "between a rock and a hard place." It looked like growing up and leaving home was not all it was cracked up to be.

Amy felt grown-up some days and then she felt like playing house with Mary as if she were her baby. When she had this mixed up thinking, she would write in the velvet diary. Putting things on paper made life clearer.

The family was ready to clamor out of the hack by the time they had bounced for an hour to get home. Turning into the lane, they passed the schoolhouse. A curl of smoke drifted from the chimney as Mr. Pierson, last year's teacher, was spending the summer in the building. Thomas hoped he would be convinced to return for another year of teaching. If not, they would be looking for some young woman who had been a good student and had completed the eighth grade already. The preference was always for a teacher who had more educational experience, which was sometimes in short supply in the valley. Amy thought maybe one day she could be a teacher, but at only five feet tall and of tiny stature, she would find it difficult to wield the switch most teachers used to keep discipline in the one-room schools. Bigger boys could pretty much do as they pleased. That's what J.J. did. Now he was on his own and Amy found that worrisome. A big brother should be around to be his sister's protector.

Sarah Ann unloaded the potluck dishes and Thomas and Link took the horses to the barn after unharnessing them from the hack. Lincoln was learning to take up the slack of J.J.'s absence on the ranch. Amy walked Mary to the house. "Get in the house and hang up those good clothes!" Sarah Ann ordered the boys. They scampered in and clumped up the stairs where each had a hook to hang his clothes. Then they were out to the fort in the dirt under the big fir to enjoy the chore-free day while it was still daylight.

Thomas sat in the big chair in the living room and Sarah Ann drew the letter from her pocket.

*Dear Tommy and Family,*

*I can hardly believe it is true, but my plans are made for our trip west. Charity and I have purchased train tickets that will take us to Baker City, Oregon. I understand there is a stage from there to the Austin House where it stops overnight. The agent tells me it is only 20 miles from there to Prairie City. It's hard to imagine a trip that took months for you in '59 can be made in a week or so. The date of departure is August 1. Thank you for the money to help. Since this is a permanent move, I must clear everything out of the little house on Clark Street. I have keepsakes to share with your children that I want to bring. If you can help with this, Charity and I will be on our way with the train reservation. I hate so to ask, but there is an extra fee for boxed belongings. We plan to get there in time to help with the harvest, canning, etc.*

*My love to you, my dear.*

*Mother Martin*

"This will make a change in our household," thought Sarah Ann. She tried to picture her home with another woman living in it. Finally she put it out of her mind. Four months from now would be the time. She would do as she saw fit now and hope her ways would meet with Mother Martin's approval.

**J.J. DID NOT FIND** a nickel a week to be adequate salary for a young man trying to be on his own. One Thursday when the stage came to a halt by the neatly-swept platform, he saw a stranger get off with a fancy valise. When he spotted J.J., he asked, "Hey kid, is there a decent place to stay around here?"

"The Prairie Hotel has just reopened after last year's fire. I hear it's a good place to stay."

"Thank ye kindly," nodded the stranger as he headed up the street.

"Hey mister, I could carry your bag for you," offered J.J.

The stranger took a long look at the boy and decided he could spare a nickel for this kid. "O.K."

The valise weighed down his arms. He traded arms, one side and then the other as he carried it up the street, wondering what could be so heavy. J.J. set the grip down in front of the counter where the man registered. His name was Clyde Stubble. J.J. waited until he collected his nickel before he tipped his cap.

Clyde Stubble looked around the little town and thought he might just find what he needed here. Stubble ran a ferry across the Snake River over on the Oregon border. Folks crossing the country could get into Eastern Oregon by using his ferry. Several days' travel could be saved for folks coming to this part of the country by using the Stubble Ferry. Right now he could run the ferry only one day a week due to lack of a crew to pull the ropes. He imagined a successful future in transportation if he could just get established and get the word out to travelers. The ferry operated in both directions so he looked to drum up business from Oregon people heading east. The country's development waved its flag before him. He took a seat in front of the hotel and fixed himself a smoke, giving him the chance to peruse the town. Tomorrow he'd rent himself a horse and ride on down to Canyon City. With slow up in the mining of that area he might find a disgruntled miner or two who wanted steadier work.

\* \* \*

The two nickels in J.J.'s pocket rubbed together as he hiked up the creek to Captain's place. He was expected in time to help irrigate the south field. A dam needed to be built on the creek to channel the water toward the field. After a good soaking, the dam was opened up to let water float on down to the river. Other places between Manwarings' and town needed water, also. The neighbors on Dixie Creek had cooperated in creating a schedule that allowed everyone to get enough water for their various crops. Some just needed to water their gardens, but Captain needed enough to grow some hay. J.J. arrived in time to see Captain bent over his shovel with some heavy sod. The two of them finished the job and guided the trickle of water to spots in the field where it would be most effective. J.J. noticed Captain breathing hard as they walked up to the house together. He felt obliged to help the old man out with the work of his place, but the nickels in his pocket sang another tune. He'd hit the road to town again tomorrow, after he helped breach the little dam.

\* \* \*

The next week Amy and Lincoln, released from chores for the afternoon, headed for the river with their fishing poles. "I hope you'll like fishing with me as much as you do with J.J," said Amy. She knew the brothers had fished together since their little boy days in Illinois. Sarah Ann used to take them to the river to fish when they first came to the ranch. When J.J. was old enough, he took Link out to the river or up Jeff Davis Creek to try their luck. "We haven't had trout for breakfast in a long time. I think we can catch enough for tomorrow morning. What do you think?"

"I think you need to be quiet. Drop your line in that calm spot under that brush," whispered Link. "I'm going upstream to J.J.'s favorite hole. Since he's not here, I think I'll take advantage and bring home his trout."

Amy hushed up, responding to her younger brother's command. *I sure wouldn't want my chatty mouth to cause an unsuccessful fishing trip*, she thought.

Amy really wanted to visit with Link, but his mind was on the catch. Typical of a boy!

"Oh wow! I snagged something." To Amy's delight the fish on her hook was a dandy. She whacked it on the head and put it in her gunnysack.

Now to rebait.

She pulled a wiggly angleworm from the tobacco can she carried. If Link were here she would get him to thread the little guy on the hook, but Amy knew how so she did it herself. With satisfaction she sat on the bank, listened to the ripples, gazed at the cottonwood trees along the bank, and dropped her line in again to the prolific fishing hole Link had shared with her. It took about half an hour for Amy to catch two more. She heard rustles in the brush behind her. Looking around, she saw Link with his bulging gunnysack. His five good-sized rainbows were added to her three. "Looks like breakfast to me," said Amy as they headed to the house.

The next morning Sarah Ann floured the fish and put them in the black skillet with some melted grease. She also cut up the extra boiled potatoes from last night's supper and fried them in the other skillet. The bigger people helped the little people at the table to take out the bones. Everyone lingered over breakfast, which was allowed because it was Sunday and the Martins didn't believe in working a full day on Sunday.

To the family's surprise, J.J. rode up on Little Brown in the afternoon. His ma gave him a hug, which he accepted graciously because she was not usually a hugger. He knew it had to be special. "I thought I'd give Mom Manwaring a break from feeding me and see how things are here."

"Well, stay for supper with us." J.J. looked relieved at the warm reception. "What have you been doing?"

"I sweep the stage platform for Mrs. Grant twice a week. I carried bags to the hotel for a stranger the other day. No steady work yet."

"Do you help Captain?"

"Oh, yeah. He says I'm working off the feed it takes for Little Brown. I'd do it anyway even if he didn't say so."

"Mom Manwaring is a good cook, but I kind of miss the way you fix some things, Ma." Sarah Ann knew she was being soft-soaped, but it was O.K.

Thomas didn't tell him he was needed on the ranch, but Lem shook his hand when he left, like he was being dismissed to go. J.J. mounted Little Brown and trotted down the road, rushing to get home before dark.

# STUBBLE'S RETURN

**STUBBLE, THE STRANGER** in town, put together a crew to run his ferry. Two knock-abouts from Canyon scheduled themselves to return to the Snake River with him. He enticed them with stage tickets, stringing their horses behind. J.J. saw them loading up on Thursday, the day the stage headed east. Stubble recognized the boy. "Hey son, next time I come through I might have a job for you. Interested?"

"Yes, sir!"

"Keep building those muscles." The men loaded up and mounted the stage. J.J. watched as they disappeared to the east.

There were no women in the stage, so the men talked rough, spit tobacco out the windows, and generally got acquainted. Stubble shared his plans, promising to pay for the work it took every time they completed a crossing. "If business is good, we'll all profit. No business, no money."

Jake, the bigger of the two, thought, *It don't sound much better than mining.*

"You'll be free to return to the mines if you want. Idaho has some pretty good ones."

Jake looked at Dave, the other recruit, with a nod and a wink.

Four months later, the ferry business was what it was, and the two men decided to move on to Idaho.

Stubble, not discouraged, supposed he needed workers willing to stay put rather than men who liked to socialize, drink on occasion, and who were greedy for money. He decided younger boys who had not developed the desire to carouse would suit his needs. For one, he remembered J.J. from his jaunt through Prairie City. There were also a couple of young bucks living on the hardscrabble ranch at the foot of Steens Mountain.

Ted and Ernest were about 16 and 17. He rode over from French Glen to have a talk about the ferry business. He painted a pretty picture of working on the river and taking home good pay. They could camp for a week at a time and then ride home to their parents' place for breaks. With their agreement, Stubble headed around the back side of Strawberry Mountain to reach the John Day Valley and to connect with the eager young man he had met there in the spring, J.J., who still needed a job.

He saw J.J. sweeping the platform at the stage stop. It looked as if he had beefed up over the summer. "Hey kid, are you still looking for another job?" he asked.

"Sure am," was J.J.'s eager reply.

Stubble described the ferry job with its pains and perks. J.J. ignored the "pains" and heard about the perks. Finally a man's job had presented itself.

\* \* \*

Captain wanted J.J. to stay until the hay was put up, which seemed fair for the summer-long room and board he had enjoyed. Mom Manwaring was nervous about him leaving, but she was getting weary of cooking and actually caring for the boy. It was time for him to step up to the adult world since he was adamant about not having any more schooling. "You must ride out to the ranch and say goodbye to your ma and pa and your brothers and sisters. It is the right thing to do," insisted Captain.

As it turned out, three weeks later J.J. took Stubble with him to meet his parents. Stubble assured them he would have concern for the boy's well-being and that he would be involved in good, honest work. The two shared dinner with the family before they headed off, taking the Logan Valley route, which passed by the headwaters of the John Day. They camped the first night at Toll Gate. J.J. remembered coming this way in '69 with the Manwaring train led by his grandfather, the captain. J.J. had been nearly nine years old. He had helped his ma over the plains with her wagon and the children after his father disappeared. J.J. thought about his life since coming to the valley. Now he thought about his new life passing back through Toll Gate. His stomach was churning, half because he was excited to go and half because he felt a twinge about leaving his family.

Stubble brewed some coffee and heated some dry biscuits the next morning before they saddled up and headed to the southeast. The camp at the top of the pass provided a cool sleeping spot. Halfway through the day, the sun did its warm-up job and J.J. broke into a sweat. So did Little Brown. Stubble rode his horse harder than J.J. had been taught to ride Little Brown. But he was part quarter horse with a big heart that did just fine at keeping up. The second night found the men camping under an outcrop of rock for protection from the wind. J.J.'s first experience with a rattler left him nervous, but Stubble dealt with the reptile handily and they slept fine after that. J.J. shared the jerky his ma had slipped in his pack. It made those dry biscuits more palatable. Midday found them looking at the Snake River from a bluff. They saw a twisty ribbon of water with a bubble of a wide spot. Stubble said, "There it is, the ford in the river where my ferry sits, just waiting to be pulled across."

# AUGUST 1876

**GRANDMOTHER MARY,** as the family referred to her, arrived with her daughter Charity at the end of August. Thomas drove the team to Austin Junction to pick them up. He and Sarah Ann agreed it would make a better welcoming than waiting another night and coming in on the stage. True to his word, Herman had found a house to share with his sister. Everyone seemed to sympathize with Charity's fate of spinsterhood, but she seemed resigned to it and content to keep house for her brother. *Maybe she will be able to keep him off the bottle and out of the pool hall*, thought Sarah Ann.

Thomas drove into the ranch late in the day. A breeze was rustling the cottonwoods and the summer heat was comfortable. He and Grandmother Mary had visited in private, reacquainting themselves. "You left Missouri at an opportune time. The War broke out. People were greatly divided. Those of us who came from the southern states were victims of the northern sympathizers. Borders under dispute created hard feelings. I nearly married again until I discovered the man was a Union soldier in plain clothes. It will be a long time before the citizens of Missouri get over the break-up."

"Sarah Ann and I have chosen not to share in political conversation. The children should grow up without prejudice about North and South. My wife came from New York and then Illinois. Her sympathies would lie with the Union, but as I said, we don't discuss it. The town is full of folks from the South. In fact, the first miners who came to the valley named their camp Dixie. The town has since been moved and renamed Prairie City. We don't need to go as far as town to get to the ranch. Charity, you can spend the night with us. Herman will come get you tomorrow. I'm wishing you good luck keeping him off the bottle," explained Thomas.

"Never mind; we'll be fine. You and Herman never did get along. On the other hand, he'll do whatever I ask. I'm his 'little sister' and he's my 'brother protector.' When we walked on the street back home, he never let anyone bother me. Maybe that's why I'm a spinster—never got bothered," replied Charity.

Thomas could see his sister had not lost her sense of humor. *That's good because she is going to need it*, he thought.

\* \* \*

Lincoln, who had been watching at the home end of the lane, came sprinting across the yard yelling, "They're coming!"

Sarah Ann called the children to come and get ready to meet their grandmother. Sarah Ann was prepared to greet Grandmother Mary warmly, but as usual, she appeared aloof in her manner, even as she walked down to embrace her mother-in-law. Amy's brief hug was barely noted in all the excitement. The ladies' trunk and valises were hauled into the living room. Pushed to the wall, the trunk would remain for emptying at a later date. The valises were carried to Amy's room for the night.

"Mary, meet your grandchildren. Amy is 14 and will be your roommate after Charity goes to town. Lincoln is our big boy. Here are Les and Lee, the twins you have heard so much about. George is next. You'll find him a big help showing you around the house, and Mary, your namesake, is the little girl toddling about, all smiles and giggles."

"Oh, Sarah Ann, they are adorable, so much prettier than the photographs you had taken. Cameras just don't do justice."

"Thomas, why don't you direct the ladies to the privy and to the porch where we wash up? Amy and I will spread out some supper. Everyone must be hungry."

Lem came to supper and got introduced all the way around. He noted Charity's height. One could tell she was Thomas's sister, tall and rather slender. Actually she was taller than many of the men Lem knew. He scooped up his stew, ate quickly, and had the good manners to leave the family alone to get acquainted.

"Pa, I like your mother," said Sarah Ann that night when they went to bed. "She really liked the boys, showed interest in what they had to say. And of course she loved Mary. Everybody does. I swear, that baby was born with a gift."

"I think it will work out fine. As I said, my mother is not afraid of work. You're going to find her good company and good help. Did you know she was born in Maryland? Then her family moved to Kentucky. They favored getting an education, just as you and I do. I think that her rearing is where I got the desire to build the Martin School," said Thomas.

"Amy is nearly a young woman now. She has enjoyed privacy in her little room. I'm just hoping sharing with your mother will sit O.K. with her," responded Sarah Ann.

"She is still a child who needs to respect her elders and I expect that is what she will do," stated Thomas.

Sarah Ann passed a little sigh as she rolled on her side to doze, hoping he was right.

\* \* \*

Two days passed and Herman did not show. They decided they would all go to the camp meeting on Sunday. Mr. Gaines, the circuit rider was expected to be there to preach. Thomas said it would be a good time to take Charity to Herman's and for his mother to see her other son. He said the ladies would also have a chance to get acquainted with some of the townsfolk. After all, this was their new home. The Prairie City residents were used to greeting strangers. Pioneers still crossed the plains to homestead land. Some still came looking for gold. Now they were greeted by a community that had survived a fire and rebuilt to its advantage. The replacement buildings looked newer and better. Prairie City had developed into an up-and-coming town.

Herman insisted he had the date wrong so that was why he had missed coming to the ranch. He was truly happy to see them and showed Charity the place he had found for her. She pictured filling it with curtains, dishes, quilts and all the things that would make it home. She gave her brother a monstrous hug, and then turned him over to his mother for another.

"So nice to meet you," gushed Mom Manwaring, wondering to herself how Sarah Ann would get along with this mother-in-law. Probably fine, she guessed, as long as she didn't criticize those children.

Turning to Sarah Ann she asked, "What do you hear from J.J.? Is he doing fine over on the river?"

"As you know, he's not much for writing, but we did get one letter. He says it's fine. I think he'll be a muscled up young man when we see him next. He spends his days pulling that ferry across the river with a rope and pulley."

"Introduce me to Thomas's mother, Sarah Ann." Kate Dearborn, her sister-in-law from the Manwaring side, was eager to get into the conversation.

"Sarah Ann and I came across the plains together. I was only sixteen. Now I'm married with three children. It's surely nice to meet you."

Kate had hardly given anyone time to make introductions before she began rattling on as usual. It rankled Sarah Ann a little bit that she was so outgoing, always laughing, with conversation that came so easily. *I'm too old to let this old jealousy rear its head. Rev. Gaines dealt with that very issue less than an hour ago*, thought Sarah Ann.

Grandmother Mary sat between Thomas and Sarah Ann on the hack seat going home. Amy was relegated to the back with the boys. Sarah Ann held Mary. "Those were a fine bunch of folks," commented Grandmother Mary. That Kate Dearborn is certainly entertaining. I think if I wanted to know anything about the people in this valley, she would be the one to ask."

Sarah Ann silently agreed with that observation. *I could tell her all about the people here, too, but I choose not to gossip about my neighbors. It is possible that they gossip about me, though*, she thought.

The Martins fell into a routine, made especially busy due to harvest of the garden and the orchard. Mr. Pierson opened school again in the middle of September. Amy, Lincoln and the twins made their way up the lane every day to attend class. Amy spent some of her time helping Mr. Pierson grade papers. Sometimes she stayed late to get it all done. The children of the neighboring homesteads filled the one room school to capacity, twenty-one pupils in all. George learned to play with little Mary while the kids were in school. For once he received enough of his mother's attention to satisfy him. His naughty streak nearly disappeared. He liked his Grandmother Mary, and she showed her fondness for him by reading stories and cutting paper figures to play parts in the various tales. He stayed much cleaner because he was not out in the dirt fort under the fir tree.

# 1877

**PROCEEDS FROM THE APPLES** went for a new bed for Amy's room. Amy no longer had to share with Grandmother Mary, but they realized she would soon be sharing with little Mary. Sarah Ann was pregnant again, so everyone knew there would be another shuffle of beds. Sarah Ann appreciated Grandmother Mary's help. She seemed to be moving more slowly with this pregnancy. Older mothers sometimes took pregnancies harder, Sarah Ann suspected. She was heavier than before, thick of waist and not just from the baby. Secretly she was hoping this would be her last child. She knew some women did something to stop babies, but she was not on intimate terms with anyone she could ask. A doctor had settled in Prairie City. He would come on horseback or in a buggy if you sent someone for him. As luck would have it, he had homesteaded on the south side of the river and his property bordered the ranch. If Sarah Ann needed him for this birth, a fifteen-minute ride would bring him.

Luckily, Dr. Doud was not needed. Labor came fast and delivery quick. Grandmother Mary and Amy helped with the birth. Thomas's mother had worked some in a hospital in Missouri and had a few tricks up her sleeve to ease the process. Sarah Ann appreciated all the help. Birthing babies when one is nearing 40 stresses a mother even if she has delivered a big family already. Sarah Ann took advantage of having the help and spent an extra day or two recovering.

Amy went back to school to help Mr. Pierson, and the boys entered school for lessons. Even George was allowed to tag along, but sitting quietly for a whole day was too difficult, and eventually Mr. Pierson said he would have to wait until next year. The days were rather quiet when school was in session. Sarah Ann nursed Eddie, her new baby boy, while little Mary enchanted everyone, especially her grandmother. George became reacquainted with his mother and found fewer reasons to cause trouble.

On September 10, 1877, a letter from Brooklyn, New York arrived on the stage mail. Sarah Ann's mother related family news, asked after the children, and then described her own health. The doctor had diagnosed a cancer, which was spreading.

\* \* \*

> *Your sister comes every day to help care for me. I do so miss Mr. Hunt. In one respect I am glad he passed last year so he would not have to share the suffering, but what a comfort he would be to me. How are you getting on with Thomas's mother? I do know how you like to do things your own way. Maybe her presence gives you time to return to the beautiful sewing you used to do. I regret I have never seen your children except in those photographs. Many families whose children went west have never even seen photographs. Luckily we are well read and educated people who have shared letters throughout the years. I am fondly your mother, Ann B. Hunt*

Sarah Ann shared the letter with Thomas, who responded with a surprise suggestion. "When you can stop nursing Eddie and have your strength back, why don't you take the train to New York and visit your mother?"

Sarah Ann gave a little gasp. She had long ago given up on her dream to visit home. Like everyone else in the valley, Oregon was now home.

"It looks like a good apple crop this year. We could use

the money for your ticket."

"Oh, Thomas," gasped Sarah Ann. She put her arms around his neck and clung there in a very long hug. This outward emotion was so uncharacteristic for them that even the children and Grandmother Mary paused to stare.

# 1878

**BEFORE THE SCHOOL TERM** ended in March, Sarah Ann finalized her plans. The presence of Grandmother Mary eased the difficult separation from the children. Thomas drove her to Baker City where she boarded the train. She carried pictures of the family, a lap robe she had made for her mother, and extra cash for food and emergencies. How different this trip east over the plains was from the first one west! She saw Indians from the safety of her car window, no threat to the passengers. She could sleep, eat, and read with no interruptions. She hoped to add to her library while in New York. The books Thomas brought her from his occasional trips to Portland were not of her choosing. She felt one had to choose her own book in order to truly enjoy it.

\* \* \*

As the train clacked along, Sarah Ann's eyes tired of reading and she slipped into a long reminiscence of her life as a young woman in New York. Ten years ago she had left Illinois with her first husband, Cody Manwaring, and her three children. Ten years before that, she had met Cody, an eighteen year old man who was sporting his first full mustache. She could even remember conversations she had with her sister, Evie, in 1859.

"How old do you think he is?" she had asked.

"Well, he must be 18," answered Evie.

"He looks older to me."

"Are you still on the lookout for a husband?" Evie asked

"Yes, the age of twenty-three is beginning to wear on me."

Sarah Ann had moved from a seamstress to an accomplished tailor at the Jenks Custom Tailors and Cleaners in Brooklyn. Her specialty was men's suits, but fitting pompous politicians was not a very pleasant occupation. She had to admit she had been looking for a handsome husband like the heroes in the novels she had read in her spare time.

Cody and his father, John Manwaring, had ridden from their home in Illinois to California and were in New York on the last leg of the trip visiting the Hunts. Sarah Ann's mother, Ann Hunt, was John Manwaring's sister.

Cody had stayed in New York and took a job at Jenks Steam Laundry. *He and I fell in love and were married. At first we lived with my parents. After J.J. was born we found our own place. Then my Amy was born and Cody's health suffered from the steam laundry work,* Sarah Ann recalled to herself.

*Then one day he said to me, "Sarah Ann, this city life is not for me. I'm missing too much work to keep us fed and housed. We need a long, happy life for the future. Let's make a change."*

*I asked if he had a plan. He did. We packed up and moved to Illinois to farm with his father.*

*My mother bid us a tearful goodbye and slipped a lovely little hand-painted perfume bottle into my pocket. Then she said, "I carried this on our voyage from England when I was fourteen years old. It has been tucked in the top drawer of our highboy for many years. I want you to have it to remind you of your childhood and your New York home."*

Sarah Ann had forgotten much of her young life, but her mother's words were as fresh in her mind as if they had been said yesterday.

\* \* \*

At the end of the train trip, she arrived to be greeted by her youngest sister and husband. Their buggy held Sarah Ann and her luggage and they headed for the family home near Brooklyn. The changes struck Sarah Ann as remarkable. There were cobbled streets where dirt roads used to be. Substantial brick buildings replaced the false front wood structures she remembered from ten years ago. Home was still recognizable, though a bit of a flutter in her chest forewarned of the excitement she felt as she stepped to the porch. Then she hugged her mother who was frail but beamed at her. "Oh Mom, I'm so happy to be here," she babbled as her words were smothered in the hug.

Catch-up conversation filled the next three days. "Oh, Mom, how wonderful things look! The fruit trees have grown beyond all expectations. I love their little green buds poking out. Is this not a warm spell for March?"

There was a humidity that Sarah Ann was no longer used to, but otherwise, the seasons were comparable to Oregon's. Purple and yellow crocuses peeked up around the yard, and the spikes of tulips poked themselves up in her mother's flowerbed. The flowerbed showed signs of neglect. Sarah Ann imagined it was due to the fact Mom did not feel well.

They spent time looking through trunks for keepsake treasures that Sarah Ann might take home to her family. "Mom, I still have the darling blue perfume bottle you gave me when I left with Cody for Illinois. It is tucked safely in the back of my dresser drawer. You know, the one that you brought from England when you were just a young girl."

"I remember. It was hand-painted and I carried it in my pocket on that crowded ship. Then we docked right here in New York where I fortunately met your father. I tell you, James Hunt was a good man. He provided for you and your sisters better than any man around here. Some men are not happy until they have a son, but your father loved his girls and saw that they could care for themselves. That's why you became a fine tailor, not just a seamstress who worked in a factory. Your first husband, cousin Cody, did not have the kind of education you did. I remember when the only work he could get was in that gas laundry. It ruined his health. I thought the fresh air of the West would be good for him. I never dreamed he'd be killed by Indians." Her mother was rattling on about things Sarah Ann had tried to push from her mind. She chose to change the subject.

"I wish you could meet Thomas, my husband in Oregon. He is gentle and kind. He never makes snap decisions. He is always thoughtful. We are of one mind about education. He built the Martin School at the top of the lane that comes to our house. J.J. quit after eighth grade, but Amy is still going as an assistant to the teacher. Next year George will be in school and Lincoln will be finished. We are determined they will be as well-educated as circumstances allow. As sad as we were to lose Cody, I now think that the children are better off than they would have been with him. Mom, Cody was so young. I thought he would grow up after we married, but he never really did. It turned me into a crabby woman keeping our family proper with his wayward ways. I've never shared these thoughts with anyone before, but being home has suddenly given me a clearer perspective." Sarah Ann was amazed at herself, unburdening to her mother like that, but with whom else could she share these intimate thoughts?

\* \* \*

The next day, her sisters came to take her to visit her father's grave in the Brooklyn Cemetery. The spot was near his parents' graves. The stones had engraved letters to identify the people who had died. Moss had begun to encroach on the parents' markers, but her father's name, James Hunt, was still clean and easy to read. Sarah Ann remembered sending some money to help pay for the headstone.

After the cemetery, they visited the Episcopal church where the family had attended services. Sarah Ann thought of the struggle for a preacher and a church building at home. Then she gave a little start. She was thinking of Oregon as home. Going home did not mean this visit to New York. It meant the big square kitchen with its long plank table where her family gathered for meals. It meant the lane to the ranch, the apple orchard across the river, and the log bridge Thomas and Lem had built to avoid fording the John Day every time they wanted to leave. Home was where she would be going in another week.

Sister Evie invited the family to dinner on Sunday. Sarah Ann drove her mother in the Hunt family buggy. They agreed to go to dinner, but not church as Mom tired easily. Being treated like a guest of honor was new for Sarah Ann, but she enjoyed not having to prepare, serve, and clean up. Mom decided to rest before starting home. Evie said, "I want you to plan to go out with me while Mom is resting tomorrow. I have something to show you over in Danfield."

\* \* \*

Sarah Ann's curiosity rose so she made plans to go with her sister. They left the house about 2:00 for the drive to the neighboring town. She could tell Evie had something to share, but she was having trouble getting out the right words.

"Let's stop at the dry cleaners," Evie announced. "The owner has fabric for sale that you might like to see."

"I really have about everything I can take back with me already."

"Well, you won't get another chance to see what is here," Evie insisted. The ladies stopped the buggy, dropped the reins over the hitching post in front, and entered the cleaners. A little bell jingled as they opened the door. The proprietor looked up briefly and nodded. The women looked over the fabric. Sarah Ann saw nothing that interested her and was ready to leave when she caught the shop owner eying her. She looked away, and then felt compelled to look at him again. Instead of a mustache, he sported a full beard. His dark eyes held a tiny twinkle that gave Sarah Ann a start. Evie nudged her and said, "Well, what do you think?"

Sarah Ann knew what she was driving at. "I think I want to leave this place before I get sick. I think I may vomit on the way home."

Evie drove to the edge of town before she pulled the buggy to a stop. "Sarah Ann, I have pondered and pondered this. I have said nothing to any member of the family. I have never spoken directly to him, but the resemblance is uncanny. You are a plainspoken person who never lies. I remember when we were little, you always fessed up to our naughty deeds. It's better to get it off your chest and take the punishment than to carry around guilt. We don't know for sure if it is he, but I learned from you long ago not to carry secrets around and I can't deal with this one alone."

Sarah Ann could see Evie's consternation. Her secret was one thing, but if that man were really her first husband, Sarah Ann's secret would be another.

She would have to put her straight-laced moral code on the line. "Evie, you are right. I can't live without knowing. It will eat away at me the rest of my life." They turned back to Danfield and stopped near the cleaners, but not right in front. Sarah Ann entered the shop again. No other customers were there. She walked straight up to the counter, "Excuse me, have you been in business long?"

"I opened this shop about five years ago."

"Forgive me for being forward, but you look very much like someone I knew many years ago. I thought you might be a relative."

"My name is Robert Main. I have no relatives around here. My family still lives in England."

Sarah Ann studied his eyes until she was quite sure that Robert Main was Cody Manwaring. Then she made her decision. "Well, thank you. I am a happily married woman from Oregon, just here to visit some family. I'll be heading back to my home in a few days. Oregon is beautiful. I really miss the country and my family. So sorry to have bothered you." She left abruptly.

Sarah Ann climbed back in the buggy. She took some time to arrange her skirts as she gathered her thoughts. She knew her decision would be life-changing, so she took a deep breath before she addressed her sister.

"Evie, I took a very close look and had a brief conversation with him. It is just a remarkable resemblance which gave me a start, but thankfully we can both put it out of our minds. He is not Cody." And, uncommon to her nature, Sarah Ann did put it out of her mind just like that.

Two days later at the end of the garden walk, she bid her mother and sisters a tearful farewell. Recovering from the blues of departure, she headed home to Thomas and her children with a special love in her breast at what a good life she had. She found herself smiling at strangers on the train. She had been wronged, but it would not ruin her outlook on life. She rose above the hurt and decided what was important to her. Her greeting to Thomas was warm and tender. He hugged her back the same. She could hardly wait to get over Dixie Pass. But Thomas had arranged for them to spend the night at Austin House where they could have a room to themselves and enjoy the pleasure of each other's company for the first time in many years. It was not time to make another baby, but it was time to share their love.

# PART II

# HOME TO THE VALLEY

**SARAH ANN AND THOMAS** turned down the lane past the Martin School on a fine April day. The orchard in full bloom promised another wonderful crop. After clacketing over the river bridge and observing the high spring run-off, they were greeted by three clamoring boys; one darling little girl, Amy, holding baby Eddie; and Grandmother Mary standing in the doorway beside Lincoln, who appeared to have grown another three inches in the past month. Supper was ready and the table conversation rattled non-stop. Sarah Ann heard about adventures of her children that she had missed. When there was a pause, she shared bits and pieces of her trip, promising the gifts from Grandma Hunt as soon as supper was over. While clearing up, Grandmother Mary whispered, "We got along just fine, but I'm glad you're home. There are so many things children need their mother for. No one else will do."

Sarah Ann replied, "I am glad to be home myself. There are things a mother needs her children for and no one else will do." They chuckled together as if sharing a joke that only mothers could understand. She continued, "I must say the changes I saw were remarkable. In ten years the railroads have become prominent throughout the country. Steel buildings have begun to replace the old wooden structures. People talk about business, manufacturing, and politics instead of rehashing the war. Our new president, Rutherford B. Hayes, is highly thought of. They say he is the most honest man in Washington. Do you know he was barely elected by one vote and the votes from Oregon were all messed up? If we hadn't straightened it out in time he would have been defeated. Imagine, me talking politics! Somehow this trip was liberating. I feel renewed."

The family noticed a sparkle in her grey eyes and animation to the straight mouth. Sarah Ann was having a good time being home and everybody knew it. After the gifts were passed around and the household had calmed down, everyone went to bed. A peacefulness greeted Sarah Ann and Thomas as they went to bed. Eddie made baby snores from his bed across the room. Sarah Ann found a favorite spot for her head in the crook of Thomas's arm and stayed there until sleep nearly overtook them and each turned away to dream his or her own dream.

The next day, the family filled Sarah Ann in on what had happened while she was gone. Most troubling was the news that Captain had taken a fall in the pasture and cracked his hip. Getting around to do his chores seemed impossible. Lincoln volunteered to help out three days a week and one of the Dearborn grandsons filled in the other three. Sundays found Mom Manwaring feeding the chickens and milking the cow. All other chores could wait.

Sarah Ann wrote J.J. about Captain's slow recovery. He decided to come home for a visit. Stubble came with him, partly for the young man's safety, as some renegade Piutes had a small band frightening ranchers in the area. Business was slow at the ferry so the men stayed several days at the ranch. Sarah Ann noticed that Stubble paid unnecessary attention to Amy. It concerned her that Amy seemed flattered by the attention. Sarah Ann felt a man of thirty had no business sparking a girl of fifteen. She sighed in relief when Stubble and J.J. rode back to Idaho and the Snake River.

The high water of the season made irrigation from Jeff Davis Creek and the John Day River easy. Lem and Thomas handled it pretty well without Lincoln's help three days a week.

* * *

Andy Larson spent the summer building the Larson School where Isham Creek met the river, close to his homestead. Other children who lived up the river joined his girls at the school, but Andy's views didn't sit well with many of the folks in the valley who were uncomfortable sending their children to his school. Andy sometimes did some of the teaching. His ideas riled the Christian folks who favored the Methodist Church. People knew he received *Truth Seeker Around the World,* a publication from W.A. Bennett, on the stage mail every couple of months. It was hard to have privacy about your mail in a small town like Prairie City. Andy was not shy about sharing his ideas, which he felt were ahead of the times. He questioned the validity of God. He quietly supported birth control. He even thought women should be allowed to vote.

People wondered how Clara McCool ended up with Andrew Larson as a husband. She went along with his ideas as she saw it as a wife's duty. His daughters were exposed to the truth-seeking, but they did not feel good about sharing the ideas with their friends. They thought their father carried his ideas too far.

\* \* \*

Finally a school was constructed in town. It had more than one room and was expected to be used for some education beyond the eighth grade. Sarah Ann and Thomas considered sending Amy to school in town, but before that could happen, Clyde Stubble arrived for another visit, uninvited by her parents, but obviously invited by Amy.

His pretense was to buy some beef yearlings to take back to the ferry where he would feed them and butcher at least one to supplement the meat supply for his camp. The men at the camp did their own cooking and probably non-existent cleaning. Sarah Ann sensed that Stubble was looking for a cook and housekeeper. She feared he was eying Amy for the job. When a dance was held in Prairie City at the Grist Mill he accompanied Amy and whirled her around. What young girl would not be entranced by dancing with a grown man? Grandmother Mary saw the concern on Sarah Ann's face. "You can't do much about it when a girl is smitten," she said.

Besides being smitten, Amy eagerly wanted to be on her own, away from the shared room with Grandmother Mary and little Mary. Just too many Marys in her life. Mr. Stubble looked like a good replacement. Amy and Stubble wanted to marry. Sarah Ann said, "Maybe after Christmas." She hoped for Amy to have a change of heart. Instead, she was pressured by her daughter to make a special gown for the wedding.

"Ma, you are a seamstress unsurpassed. Please make me a beautiful gown," pleaded Amy. Sarah Ann gave in. Thomas said they could be married at the ranch, so plans were made for a March wedding.

\* \* \*

Before the wedding, Captain took a turn for the worse and passed in January. Beloved by many of the people in the valley, he had a well-attended service followed by the burial. Fortunately a mid-thaw softened the ground enough to dig the grave. A free will collection was taken for the tombstone of the man who had brought so many settlers to the community. Many folks who died in those years had graves marked with a wooden cross only. Some were marked with hand-engraved stones. Occasionally a stonecutter was available to do a professional job. Captain's maker was nearly four feet tall, a four-sided affair with etchings on three sides and the name and dates chiseled on the fourth. Sarah Ann and Thomas thought it was overdone, more ornate than the man himself would have chosen. The work was done in Portland and the stone was shipped up the river to The Dalles and brought home to Prairie City in a wagon. As sometimes happens in long distance communications, a mistake was made. John Manwaring lay beneath a stone that said he was Joseph Manwaring. The money had been spent and there was no more to send it back for a correction. It was a fine looking stone, the tallest in the cemetery, and people who visited it just explained it really marked Captain John Manwaring.

* * *

The wedding took place at the ranch in March as planned. Amy's dress enhanced her dainty body and Sarah Ann tailored a warm cape of her own design for the ride to Idaho. Thomas signed the marriage certificate that swore Amy to be fifteen and of legal age to marry. Several close friends came; two signed as witnesses and as luck would have it, the circuit rider, Rev. Hagan, was on hand to perform a ceremony. Sarah Ann was pleased with this. A religious ceremony seemed more special than standing before a judge to make marriage legal. J.J. came with Clyde Stubble for the wedding and was prepared to drive the couple back to Idaho Territory in the wagon. Sarah Ann felt comforted that J.J. lived at the Stubble camp where Amy would soon be cook and housekeeper and no doubt a mother before a year was over.

"Yes, Amy is a lovely bride," Sarah Ann answered a comment made by Amy's friend Rhoda. "You're right, I will miss her greatly."

The boys were all slicked up for the ceremony and beginning to realize their sister was leaving and going to the same place J.J. had. They thought Idaho Territory was where everyone went to make new starts, sort of like crossing the plains in reverse. But they were more concerned with immediate matters. "Ma, can we eat now?" they asked together.

The food was set out on the long table for the guests to help themselves. Many weddings were potluck affairs, but Sarah Ann had chosen to make the whole meal herself. Thomas brought one of the hams in from the smokehouse and Grandmother Mary helped fix things to go with it. "I thank God every day for Grandmother Mary's help," thought Sarah Ann.

"Let's let Amy and Clyde go first. That is the proper thing to do at a wedding. Then you boys may help yourselves," explained Sarah Ann.

Thomas said a few words of congratulations and Rev. Hagen said a blessing on the food. Lem whispered something in Amy's ear that made her blush. Then they all gathered round and filled their plates with food. Sarah Ann brought a cake from the back porch where it had been kept cool so the fancy icing did not slide down the sides. George and little Mary looked with big eyes. They did not know their ma could make anything so fancy. Again, everyone had to wait for Amy and Clyde Stubble before they could have their pieces. Mom Manwaring hugged Amy and shook Clyde's hand and gave everyone a big smile, the first since before Captain's funeral.

The married couple and J.J, the driver, planned to take the long way home so they could stop at the Austin House for the night. By mid-afternoon they were packed up with extra food in a big basket and blankets bundled around. Sarah Ann and Thomas waved from the porch. Little Mary shed tears to see her Amy leave. Most of the guests drove off shortly after. The Martin family attacked the job of cleaning up. Tomorrow was another workday with never-ending chores to be tackled. There was always time to think while one worked, but Sarah Ann had never lingered over her thoughts. Since returning from New York she sported a new philosophy of making each day worthy of her efforts. Worry about the past, like crying over spilled milk, was a pointless waste of time.

# THE NEW PHILOSOPHY
# 1880

**SARAH ANN** was hard-pressed to explain the new philosophy that had taken over her thoughts and feelings. She was more affectionate with Thomas. He liked the growing attention, the special looks and the twinkling eyes. She and her husband discussed more than the ranch work and the children's education. Thomas was admired in the community for his thoughtful approach to matters of the valley. He contributed to the church fund regularly. Sometimes he drove to Canyon City to listen to the county commissioners. They listened to his ideas and discussed things that might be taken to the legislature.

"Pa, I think fifteen is just too young to marry. Not just because of Amy, but because all girls need more time to grow up. They cut off the chance for more education if they marry so young. I understand no young woman wants to be an old maid. That drives them to marry young. But if the law didn't allow it until they were sixteen, they would be just that much older, more mature." Sarah Ann expressed herself on a topic she had been thinking about.

"I agree with you. As always I am in favor of more education for boys and girls, gives them opportunities they otherwise don't get."

"How would the county commissioners feel about such a law?" Sarah Ann posed.

"Why don't I bring it up at the next meeting? Nothing says our ideas from this valley should not become law. In fact, I imagine we would not be the first county to propose a change to the law."

From the seeds of that conversation, the proposal reached Salem and eventually the ballot. Sarah Ann was pleased about it as well as pleased about being in a family way one more time. Pleased for a love child instead of a duty child. Why the delay until after her 40th birthday? No matter; Sarah Ann looked forward to another baby in the house.

* * *

Evelyn was born in 1880. She was named for Sarah Ann's sister. "When I was growing up, my baby sister was Evelyn. Now as the boys and Mary grow up, their baby sister will also be Evelyn," she told Pa. It was fine with him because he didn't much care for *his* sister's name, Charity. Besides, she was an old maid and he would not want his little girl to grow up an old maid.

The birth had been her most difficult. Dr. Doud was called. When he finished, he said, "Sarah Ann, you have had enough babies. I'm going to tell Thomas the same thing. In fact I'm going to give him some information on avoiding another pregnancy. You have been a healthy woman. I want to see you remain healthy so you can care for this wonderful family." Sarah Ann knew the doctor was right, but the end of childbearing is the end of something a woman treasures, even if she is worn out, and she had mixed feelings. "Sarah Ann, I can stop you from getting pregnant again and you will never know there is a difference. You will feel the same, but you will have no fear of getting pregnant. Let me finish my work of repair after this delivery. You will recover with no worries regarding our conversation," Dr. Doud told her.

"Go ahead," nodded Sarah Ann. She knew the doctor's advice was correct. As he worked, she dozed off and had a little dream of Mrs. Larson, who lived up the river. She only had two children. Mr. Larson read everything D.M. Bennett wrote and it was known that he supported women's rights and birth control. These were issues discussed in the newspapers from the East. They were issues not discussed in this valley. The folks in this valley were Victorian, Christian, and hard working. Their morals were unquestionably right. Those rabble-rousers like D.M. Bennett deserved the stints in jail they were receiving, according to them. Sarah Ann woke from her dream with the Larsons on her mind. "Dr. Doud, I'm over 40 years old. No one will expect me to have more children and they need not know why."

"Exactly right!" Dr. Doud believed his job here was finished. The baby daughter nursed at her mother's breast. The mother would surely not suffer any bad effects from another delivery.

Meanwhile, Thomas had saddled Doc's horse.

"What do I owe you?" asked Thomas. Then he remembered why the doctor was there and asked, "How is Sarah Ann? "

"She's fine. I'll send you a bill," he replied, knowing that Thomas Martin would pay his debts. He opened the pasture gate and rode to the south and his home at the base of the foothills leading to Strawberry Mountain.

**A FEW WEEKS LATER** Sarah Ann began putting her thoughts in order in a journal:

*My Thoughts while Lying in Bed*

*It is 1880 and Evelyn has entered the world. The doctor said no more children for me. It could have been the beginning of the end, but instead it is the beginning of something new. I'll spend a few extra days in bed after the birth of this lovely little girl. I'll nurse her and become acquainted in a very special way. Life has a lot to offer. As I calculate the good and the bad of my life, I know the good outweighs the bad. Maybe things look good now that I had not recognized before. Long ago I was consumed with worry about being a spinster. How foolish that had been! Yet it was like something inborn. In my mind I know one can still have a wonderful productive life without a husband and a gaggle of children, but in my heart I do not want my two daughters to be spinsters.*

*I discovered I was living with a lie. I didn't know it. Now I do know it, but it is nobody's business but my own, and I can live with it happily tucked far away, like the tiny perfume bottle in the back corner of the highboy. It is not written down, so it lives with me and dies with me. The story is much more interesting than the hurtful truth. I kill the hurtful truth now, forever! My treasures fill a list from here to eternity and they are here in this valley. My list begins with Thomas, my bearded husband, an honest man, committed to family and future, and committed to me. Thomas is also committed to the land. His intelligence tells him that business and industry are destined to come, but without land he sees no future for himself or his family.*

*I believe I must think toward the future for Evelyn and maybe even Eddie. My Manwaring children are making lives for themselves. Actually their Stubble's Ferry connections put them in business. Everyone in the West needs a farm to feed the family, but the income is made from business. But, to Thomas these are just sidelines. Owning land and making it our business is what he sees for the future.*

*Our life measures up very well with the other families in the valley. We save money, only spending what we need to expand the ranch and planning for our small trips and adventures. The orchard money is a fine example. The boys will soon be big enough to do their share of the work. Thomas has trained them to know what to do. When boys are small, patience is required to see that they learn. These boys reap the rewards of a father determined to train them up properly. Whether Thomas agrees or not, I see my responsibility with Mary and Evelyn to train them to be as modern as women can be today. I think the time will come when women do not depend on their husbands for every need. I think the time will come when women will own property and work at jobs other than cooking for families. Right now women are powerful in church and charity work. Some day they will even vote.*

*Thomas hired the Davies girl to come help out during my recovery. She is good help in the kitchen and also good at seeing that the children are occupied. I know there will be a mountain of laundry waiting when I get out of this bed. I should have trained the twins to do the laundry, but they are probably too young to do a good job. Maybe I could get Thomas to do it. Then he would soon consider one of the new washing machines I*

> *saw working in New York. If we got one of those, we would be the first in the valley to have one. If that happened, everyone would know it and think I was putting on airs. I don't care. Every family should have a washing machine. Washboards are a thing of the past except here in the West.*
>
> *My feeling of envy came home with me from the trip. I don't know why, but now I want things I didn't want before. I'm not afraid of the ranch work that we do, but we must look to the future or we'll be left like those Southerners after the war, clinging to poor overworked land. I read about it during my trip home on the train. I think we need a newspaper in the house on a regular basis so we can keep up on the world's doings. In order to do all the reading I plan on I will probably need reading glasses. The print in my Bible seems smaller than it used to. There are a lot of things to talk over with Pa when he comes in to see Evelyn and me today.*

"Ma, we did ourselves proud with this one. She is sure special," beamed Thomas when he came to the house for dinner. "We're all anxious for you to get back to the dinner table with us. That rowdy crew misses its ma."

"Just give me a couple more days. This lying in bed is restful, but I know there are things that need doing."

"I was thinking, we could keep the Davies girl a while longer to help out until you are back to full strength."

"Maybe for a week or so," answered Sarah Ann. "I'm not sure I will work well with another in the kitchen. I remember how difficult it was to get used to your mother when she first came."

"You can decide, but Doc says to avoid heavy lifting, so I plan to make that happen as much as possible."

"You are a dear husband," said Sarah Ann. "Pa, there are some other things I've been thinking while lying here. I want to bring a newspaper into the house. These children need to grow up knowing what is going on in the world. When I was East, people were talking about a lot of things besides farms and crops. Factories and businesses are springing up all over the country, but also about education. There's more to it than just what they learn in the Martin School."

"Well, don't sell the Martin School short!"

"I'm not selling it short. It is wonderful that you built it so J.J., Amy, and Lincoln could take advantage of it. Now the twins, George, Mary, and soon Eddie will go there. I am thankful for the school. I'm just saying there is more to learn."

"Give me a little time to cogitate on what you're saying." Thomas rose from the side of the bed and went to the kitchen to eat with the family.

*He always needs time to think about things. I know that. I've had several days to "cogitate" as he puts it. I tell myself to be patient while this good man "cogitates." Evelyn, I think it's time your mother got on her feet. Oops, I feel dizzy, maybe just feet over the edge of the bed for now. Doc is right, no more childbirth for me. I think Evelyn and I will take a nap.*

A squeak as the door opened just a little way reminded Sarah Ann of when George was little and wanted to peek in at Mary. Only this time it was Eddie coming to peek at Evelyn. "Hello, Eddie, how are you?"

"Ma, can I come in? Bett Davies said I had to stay out," pleaded the little voice.

"Do you want to look at Evelyn?"

"No, want to see you."

"Eddie, go ask Bett to come in and talk to me." The little boy minded his mother and went to look for Bett Davies.

"Bett, I'm feeling much stronger. You can let the children come in as long as they ask first."

Bett agreed. "If that's what you want Miss Sarah Ann."

"I do. I've been too long without the joy and aggravation of those children."

Evelyn became the family's new entertainment, especially for young Mary who finally had a baby to play house with, just as Amy played house with her when she was a baby.

**ONE DAY WITHOUT WARNING,** Grandmother Mary said, "Sarah Ann, I'm not feeling too well this morning. Could little Mary bring up a cup of tea to our room?" Sarah Ann was surprised at the request but sent little Mary hustling up the stairs. In the middle of the morning, Sarah Ann climbed the stairs to check on Mary who was pale and clammy.

"Mary, Mary, are you all right?"

"I think I have the grip," she weakly replied.

"Let me get you another blanket," Sarah Ann offered. Mary seemed to warm up and doze off after Sarah Ann covered her with the warmest wool blanket in the house. The blanket was made from wool they had carded from the sheep Thomas used to keep before getting seriously into the cattle business. A wool blanket was warmer than the many quilts the family usually slept under. Sarah Ann decided to let her sleep and went to the kitchen to deal with the chicken Lincoln had just butchered. She put parts to cook for broth and rolled out some flour noodles. She cut the dough into strips and hung them over a line in the kitchen to dry. She felt sure Grandmother Mary would be ready for chicken and noodles for supper.

Sarah Ann sent Thomas up to check on his mother. He found her, not clammy, but burning with fever. They carried water to her room and sponged her off to bring the fever down. When the fever broke, she sat up and appeared to have recovered. She let herself be helped down the stairs, wearing a robe, and joined the family for chicken and noodles. Mostly, she ate the broth. Dr. Doud came the next afternoon. He left some medication to help Mary feel better, and prescribed as much chicken soup as she could eat. Sarah Ann put herself to the task of making soup. She felt better doing something constructive. Mary seemed to be her old self after medicine and soup, but Sarah Ann thought her speech was slower and her quick glances had slowed. Things the children did passed by without her notice. Mary spent more time in the rocking chair with handwork in her lap, untouched.

\* \* \*

Mary Martin, an old woman whose body just wore out, passed in 1880. Thomas had a professionally turned stone erected in her honor. Herman and Charity thanked Thomas for taking care of such a nice stone as they had no money for such. After the graveyard service, the children walked from the cemetery to town, where Thomas later picked them up in the wagon.

George, an impressionable eight-year-old, saw his Uncle Herman leave the saloon after the funeral. Herman staggered a bit on his way down the street. One of George's classmates in town for the day said, "There goes the town drunk."

"That's my Uncle Herman," George retorted.

"Well, he's still the town drunk." George's ears burned bright red as he tore down the street looking for his pa. This embarrassment was something little George would never forget.

\* \* \*

*Could this really be 1880?* Sarah Ann thought. Evelyn was born, Mary died. She knew her own mother would soon be gone. She and Thomas would then be the older generation. This idea stuck in her craw. *I'll make the 1880s count for something,* she thought.

"Pa, I think we should subscribe to the newspaper," she told Thomas.

"The news we get in the paper is pretty outdated," he commented.

"Better than no news at all," countered Ma.

"I suppose, but I think you may need glasses to read the small print."

"So be it! I can use them to sew with, too." Sarah Ann would not be dissuaded.

"When we go to town on Saturday, take a look at Marsh's for some spectacles and we'll buy them." Thomas gave in to

Sarah Ann most of the time. She only made responsible requests, nothing worth arguing about.

"I think I heard that the *Oregon State Journal* was going out of business. What paper would you want to read?" asked Thomas.

"I've heard *The New Northwestern* is interesting reading."

"Where did you hear about that one? I don't know a thing about it," said Thomas.

"Mrs. Grant at the postal office mentioned it. It's published by Abigail Duniway. Her brother publishes that other paper in Portland. She has been linked with Susan B. Anthony. I just think it might be interesting reading," repeated Sarah Ann.

Thomas raised his eyebrows, but it was not noticeable because he had on his hat and was headed out the door to ride his big-bodied white horse to town. Charger had been a tough colt to break but had turned into the best cow horse Thomas ever had. He was raw-boned and tough as nails. He could move cattle all day and never look tired. Of course, every horse perked up on his way home to the barn where the saddles came off and the feed was plentiful. Thomas and Charger headed for the mail service in town. It still came in on Thursdays as it had for the past ten years.

Thomas wanted to do some banking also. The bank established in town housed a small complement of safety deposit boxes. He thought one of those boxes would be a safe place to keep the deeds he held to the various properties he had homesteaded and purchased. On his way past Marsh's he stopped for a sack of penny candy for the children, a treat for after supper. Eddie's sweet tooth was the most demanding in the family.

"Candy is not good for that boy," fussed Sarah Ann when Thomas returned from town.

"I can't help it. I just have a soft spot for that little guy when he whines for sweets."

"I think we are just getting older and tired of being disciplinarians. It may be a good thing Evelyn is the last child. I think our determination is slipping."

"Not slipping very far!" countered Thomas. "Where are those boys? I see about a dozen chores that didn't get done while I was gone." Thomas stepped out of the house to return to his quiet but forceful method of discipline. Boys' heads appeared from various spots and the barn got mucked out, the pigs were slopped, and Charger was wiped down after his saddle was hung up. Lem and Lincoln came in from the field and all was in order for supper. Young Mary set the table as Eddie did his best to bother her. She popped him with a dishtowel, a trick she had learned from her brothers. It was more fun to be on the giving end than the receiving end of a dishtowel pop. Eddie cried and ran to Sarah Ann who showed him very little sympathy. She did share one of her stern looks with Mary, however.

\* \* \*

"Ma look!" yelled the twins from the front porch. Smoke rising in a spiral could be seen from the direction of town. Was this a repeat performance? Three miles was a long way to see smoke, so they knew there must be a big fire. Thomas, Lem, and Lincoln decided to saddle up and ride to town to investigate. They found townsfolk creating a bucket brigade from the creek to stop the flames. The men stepped in to help. Many of the current workers were already exhausted. Five businesses were burned out, but the water brigade had stopped the fire before the whole town was destroyed. Still standing on the north side of the street was the butcher shop with its stone bull's head on guard. Much to Thomas's relief, the bank was untouched. Smoke had damaged the pool hall, but most of the patrons smoked anyway, so they would soon get used to the smoky smell. Marsh's was burned out. The post office and stage stop were badly charred. The sawmill would need to rebuild. The men from the Martin Ranch found things a mess.

"It was quite a fire with a lot of damage," Thomas reported. "Everybody looked beat tonight, but I reckon the pioneer spirit will take over and folks will clean up and rebuild. Saturday has been set as a clean-up day. I think the boys can go along and work with the rest of us. The ladies will potluck a dinner meal to keep us all going." Folks automatically knew they would devote a day's work to the cleanup of Prairie City.

On the way home, Thomas brought up a new subject with Sarah Ann. "Zeke Cleaver plans to refurbish the meat market. Although his business was not damaged by this fire, he figures this is a good time to spruce up his building and expand the facilities he has for his butcher shop. He asked if I would be interested in owning a portion of the business in exchange for financial help to enlarge."

Sarah Ann registered surprise in her eyes. Owning a business in town presented problems—many trips to town no matter what the weather, keeping ledger books, being aware of people's finances. She knew many folks bought on the cuff when they were short of cash. "Pa, I can think of disadvantages. Tell me the good things about doing this."

"I was thinking that I've been buying property with the boys' futures in mind. This might be a place for Lincoln to work when he finishes school. I don't have a piece of property in mind for him. The size to which we have expanded the ranch is about right to handle. If we buy more land and cattle, we will need a larger full time crew. Cooking for more hands would mean hired help for you since Amy and my mother are gone. Maybe you would rather help keep books than keep house, now that you have a newfound interest in newspapers and politics." Thomas was making a point in a half- kidding manner.

"When are you planning to let him know?"

"Actually, I already did." They rode home in silence. Sarah Ann was forming her ideas and words before laying them on her husband. His business judgment was not bad, but his actual decision without consulting her was <u>very</u> bad. She was contemplating just how to let him know the nature of their relationship going forward.

# SEPTEMBER 1883

**LINCOLN'S LAST YEAR** in the Martin School meant decisions needed to be made. He could go to town to the Prairie City School for another year. Thomas thought he could go to school and then work the rest of the day in the butcher shop. He was not prepared to foot the bill to send him to the academy in Portland.

"I'm not very keen on the butcher shop. Killing animals and dressing them out has always been my least favorite job on the ranch," Link told his mother who understood his feelings, but Thomas had made the butcher shop decision with Link's future in mind. He treated all the Manwaring children as if they were his own, but there was a little difference when it came to money investments. Sarah Ann thought Lincoln would be very wise to follow his pa's plan. Link thought the plan was too rigid. The old issue of parents knowing what is best and children not accepting the fruits of that knowledge reared its ugly head again. Sarah Ann sighed in her wisdom and chose not to discuss it right now.

Lincoln finished his eighth grade year at Martin School. He helped out on the ranch during the spring and summer. Thomas sent him to town one day a week to learn the meat market business from Zeke Cleaver. The job wasn't too bad and it did give the boy some variety. He was paid 25 cents for every day he worked. Lincoln was sliding into the job market more easily than his brother J.J. had when he finished eighth grade. So, taking the year of high school offered in town seemed agreeable for the next school year, and Lincoln became a part time butcher on the side.

Sarah Ann saw that he was growing up in so many ways. The children seemed to reach that point before she was ready for it to happen, but in her maturity, she came to accept it gracefully. J.J. was successful with Stubble in the ferry business. Just as expected, Amy would deliver Sarah Ann's first grandchild in a matter of weeks. "When Lincoln decides to leave, he will be better prepared than the other two," she thought to herself.

Lincoln passed the competency tests to leave higher school. Begrudgingly, he worked full time in the butcher shop. Sarah Ann spent one day each week in town checking on the sales, counting the money, and recording the credits in the ledger book. All records were written in pencil as pen and ink was too messy to have on the counter in the meat market. She put the totals in ink at the bottom of each column so amounts could not be changed with an eraser and still be accurate. As more people saw the advantage of the experts cutting their meat, the business flourished.

"Hey, Lincoln, how about some sausage?" a customer asked.

"Yes sir, Mr. Waldon," Lincoln hopped to filling the order from the big cooler where the meat was kept. Sausage was tricky to make because everyone liked a different spice. Finally the blend Lincoln and Thomas considered the best was written down and the recipe, always the same, became popular.

As Waldon left with his pack of sausage, a stranger entered the shop.

"My name is Boynton. I live in John Day. Last week I heard about the quality of the meat sold here. I've come up to give it a try. We are entertaining a gentleman from Portland who is interested in investing in this area. I'm aiming to show him what this valley has to offer."

Lincoln was not used to hearing so much about a purchase, but he sensed this was an important order. He was alone in the shop, so he made a suggestion of a fine beef roast and even explained how his mother would choose such a piece of meat. Mr. Boynton seemed agreeable, so the meat was weighed out and a nice profit was registered in the book for his ma to see.

On the days Sarah Ann came to town to do her bookkeeping, she took Eddie to school for the day and left Evelyn with Lem. Since Lem had taken a fall from his horse last year, he favored a bad leg. He favored a day off heavy ranch work, also. Sarah Ann believed watching Evelyn for the day saved the leg. Lem's fondness for the little girl showed through his actions. The two would feed the chickens, pull some weeds or hoe in the garden--getting it ready for planting. Evelyn kept him moving from task to task until she napped. Sarah Ann knew Lem probably napped, too. Thomas might come in from the field to find the two of them quiet in the house. He found Lem a better worker the next day, maybe because of the rest or maybe because little Evelyn had worn him out. Sarah Ann chuckled to herself, realizing men do not know the extent of a woman's job.

*The New Northwestern* editorials interested Ma. She read them religiously. She became as addicted to this newspaper as Andy Larson was to *The Truth Seeker Around the World*. Not many folks knew she was reading it. Unlike Andy's periodical, this one did not question God or most standard morals. It did question the fairness of women's roles in Western society. Sarah Ann agreed that women have much more to offer than raising babies. Too many ignore the completion of women's work when the children ride off to lives of their own. What's left? Sarah Ann was determined she would still have a worthwhile life. J.J. and Amy were gone and she knew Lincoln would be soon. The right opportunity would present itself and he would go.

Five Martin children still attended the Martin School, which grew every year. They made up less than a quarter of the total census. The teacher usually had a helper, some previous student who showed promise with reading and numbers. Les and Lee always did their work at school. They were not remarkable students, but they had a good understanding of what the teacher was requiring. The twins supported one another, which gave them the confidence of never being alone. They would not be asked to be class helpers, but Sarah Ann and Thomas were already discussing sending them to Portland to the academy when they finished the schooling that was available to them in the valley. "I think they will do fine because they have each other as companions. I don't think they will be homesick," reasoned their ma.

"Well, we still have a few years to think about it," said Thomas. Sarah Ann knew he would think it over carefully before making a decision.

"We can expect Amy for a visit this year," said Sarah Ann. Amy did correspond with her when she had time. Sarah Ann was eager to meet her granddaughter. Amy had named her Ann after Grandma Hunt. Sarah Ann was pleased with the name choice. It made her feel as if Amy counted her mother's family as special.

\* \* \*

J.J. came with Amy as Stubble had to tend to ferry business. They stayed for a week. What a joy to hold a little baby again. Evelyn showed her jealousy, as she had never had to share her ma's attention before. She chased and followed Lem around as he limped from chore to chore. Evelyn did warm up to Amy before she left for home and gave her a big goodbye hug.

Sarah Ann's fears were realized when Lincoln came and expressed his desire to go to Idaho with J.J. and leave his job at the butcher shop. J.J. had assured him there would be work for a strong young man, especially one who was expert in cutting meat. The ferry fort was growing and Lincoln should get in on the ground floor, according to J.J.

"J.J., you sound just like Stubble. Has this move been everything you expected?" asked his ma. Thomas sat silently and stayed out of the conversation.

"Sure, Ma; it's been great," J.J. lied. The scars on his hands and the stoop in his walk told a different story. His pride would not permit him to share the real rigors of his life. Sarah Ann sighed, realizing one more child was about to leave her nest. At least this one had some preparation for his future.

Thomas finally entered the conversation. "Giving some notice to the meat market that you will be leaving would be the right thing to do."

"You're right, Pa. I know right from wrong. J.J., how much time do I have to get there and still get the ferryman's job that is available?"

"I think the current one is leaving the end of the month. If you were there in three weeks, you could learn the ropes."

"I'll be there." Sarah Ann could see Lincoln's excitement. She knew missing another child would put a crack in her heart, but when the first one left, she thought her heart would break. Now she knew it would not. A strong woman with emotions in check. That was Sarah Ann.

# LES, LEE, AND GEORGE

**REPLACING THE RIVER BRIDGE** needed to be done this spring. Thomas farmed land on both sides of the river. Buttercups popped up first near the banks, and later along the hillsides. A little later, yellow bells and bird bills dotted the hill pastures. It was time to move the cattle across the river and into the hill pastures. Les and Lee rode twin horses, pinto ponies. They saddled their own horses and rode with the men to move the cattle. George begged to go along. Thomas gave in, although George needed help to saddle up and needed to be trained on how to chase an errant cow. Thomas knew he needed to learn, so along he went.

The cows bawled at their calves and at one another. The hillside grass provided a tender treat and the cattle moved out as if they knew this too, stopping to eat as soon as they were through the gate. They had to be herded along so the whole band could get into the pasture. Les and Lee rode ahead to get the head cows going. Old cows remember where they have gone in previous years, so driving them is actually pretty easy. George was delegated to the rear with Lem to be sure there were no stragglers. It was a good place for the little guy to learn, but also the dustiest place to be. As usual, he would get home the dirtiest in the bunch.

Thomas praised George. "You did a good job. I expect you to be a great cowman one day. You can help me run the ranch." The little boy's chest puffed up with importance. When his pa gave a compliment, it was never idle words. It meant something.

Sarah Ann saw the effects of the praise and knew George was coming into his own after taking a back seat to the twins for too many years. She saw he had a twinkle in his grey eyes. She also noted that his interest lagged at school. Reading and numbers came easily enough, but he could hardly be bothered with writing. George sensed no reason for punctuation. His papers were run-on masterpieces. They told what he wanted to say with never a period or a capital letter. George spoke the same way, run on without a breath. Sarah Ann knew it was his way of getting his words in edgewise when the twins monopolized the conversations.

Sometimes George spent time with Mary. They were close in age and had many interests in common. They played fort together, but now the role of ladies occupied some of the time. George had a chance to let Mary share her ideas of what the fort should be. More time was spent preparing make-believe meals and less time fighting the Indians who threatened them. George could remember when they went to the real fort for protection; Mary could not. Sarah Ann saw that times were changing. Fear of Indians was not the hot political topic it once had been.

Thomas took Sarah Ann with him to Portland. The chance to ship cattle there for sale was worth investigating. One had to decide if the cost of shipment would offset the profit to be made here where the demand was higher than eastern Oregon. They stayed at the new hotel, *The Imperial*. The owner of the hotel was looking for investors to share in the decorating costs in return for a bit of the profit from the business. Thomas found himself tempted again to enter a new business. The money earned from the meat market had proved it to be a good investment. Sarah Ann tried to take a serious look at this idea. What really appealed to her was the opportunity to come to Portland a couple of times a year and take advantage of what a city had to offer. Restaurants and musical shows were enticing. Sarah Ann thought this venture might turn into something special. Thomas made only a small contribution to the decorating. He was reluctant to venture into a business he knew so little about. He would do nothing to jeopardize the ranch, the future for his boys. He had property in mind for Les, Lee, and George. He had yet to acquire a place for Eddie, but that was a long way off.

He expected his daughters to marry well and have no need for property. In his head, Thomas was figuring it all out as usual. Sarah Ann could "read his mind" about his desires for the children. She hoped they would all work out for him. She still remembered how distraught she was when the Manwaring children had chosen their own paths to follow.

\* \* \*

Tending the Manwaring place after Captain died was too difficult for Mom Manwaring. Jim Hardy had property near her place, and soon he courted the widow. After a respectable year, they married and joined their properties. Jim moved into

Mom Manwaring's house. Both were getting older and found farming hard work. About all they could do was make enough to feed themselves. Mom Manwaring's children shared food from their farms. Sarah Ann, as an ex-daughter-in-law, did not feel obliged to contribute. Mom Manwaring had always been critical of the woman who was once married to her son. Sarah Ann wondered how she would feel to know the truth, but she had decided that truth of her secret would never be shared. *I'm a strong enough woman to carry that secret to the grave,* she thought to herself. So, the Hardys got by like so many other people, without extra help from the Martins.

* * *

When it came to the Methodist Church, the Martins were very charitable. They made a sizeable donation and devoted time to the raising of the building. It was actually a remodel of the school. Land donated from the Marsh place was the home for the church and a new school building was constructed on the school site.

Plans for the church included a steeple with a place for a bell to hang. Purchasing the bell was delayed until the rest was paid for. Then a bell fund was started. The minister who came made it a point to travel to every home and farm in the area. Nearly everyone attended Sunday services. Even Andy Larson allowed his family to come, but they lived quite a way from town so their attendance was irregular. The social functions surrounding the church enticed many for potluck dinners. Thomas, however, believed attendance at a weekly worship service was paramount to raising a pious family and now that the church was established, he insisted they attend every Sunday. Sarah Ann had grown up in an Episcopal church on Long Island and also believed attendance was very important. Only Lem stayed home when the family harnessed up the team and drove off to worship.

# AUGUST 1886
# MORE EDUCATION

**"I'M NOT SURE** I want to go to Portland to school," said Lee. The occasion for the statement was the notice that he and Les had passed the two-year high school competencies. Thomas had made plans without consulting the boys. Les was more receptive than his brother. Throughout the years he had shown more willingness to venture forth into new territory. Leaving home did not sound scary to him. Lee, on the other hand, was more of a homebody.

"We expect you boys to take advantage of this offer. More schooling will hold you in good stead no matter what you decide to do in life. After you finish the two-year program, the ranch will be waiting for you. After you grow up and marry, you will be able to purchase the land from me in exchange for working it." Thomas was stubborn after he made up his mind. The boys knew an argument would be fruitless. So in September they gathered their gear and made ready for their new adventure. Thomas took them to the train in Baker City and decided to ride the rails with them to be sure they were established in a place to live and registered in the appropriate classes. Les and Lee were instructed to write to their mother every week, Les one week and Lee the next. Thomas then made his way to the Imperial Hotel to check on his investment. The decorations looked wonderful, very high class. He knew Sarah Ann would approve. Thomas's hope was to make enough with this venture to pay the twins' tuition. He stopped to see them on his way out of town the next day. Lee looked homesick, so Thomas left quickly, not giving him a chance to express how miserable he was.

\* \* \*

Arriving in Baker City, Thomas went to the livery to pick up his team and pay the fee for their keep. In Portland he had purchased a couple of issues of the newspapers from the stand in the hotel. He thought Sarah Ann would be interested in what was in print in the "big city." Thomas appreciated Sarah Ann's ideas. He thought maybe someday women would be voting. If they were all as intelligent as his wife, the country would not suffer from their votes. He never expressed these thoughts to his cronies in town or to the council members at the church. Their Victorian ideas took precedence over any new thoughts on morals or politics.

Thomas watched Sarah Ann as she reared Evelyn. She treated her differently from how she had treated Amy and even Mary. Sarah Ann had grown up with a strong instinct about being an old maid. That concern had encouraged her to marry her cousin, thinking no other man was available to a twenty-three year old woman. She thought Amy was too young, but again she did not want her to be an old maid. Her feelings about Thomas's sister, Charity, were very clear. She felt pity because she was a spinster. Thomas blessed her every day for seeing to his brother Herman, who could not resist the drink. The lengthy drive home gave him a lot of thinking time. Maybe he would hatch another plan for ranch expansion. He needed to give some thought to Eddie's future.

"Eddie has a temper," Thomas began talking to himself. His team twitched their ears, but the words did not apply to what they had been trained to do, so the horses just continued down the road.

Thomas practiced his speech aloud, remembering how he had tried to train J.J. He thought he would try something different this time. "Eddie, it's time for you to behave better. Next year when you are in second grade, you will be too big to act like a baby. So, we are going to practice holding your temper at home. If you get into trouble at school next year, you will be in big trouble at home. If you are in doubt, just ask J.J. the next time you see him. He can tell you it is smart to stay out of trouble."

When Thomas drove the team down the lane and over the bridge, he could see the light from the oil lamp in the kitchen window. Sarah Ann was waiting. He felt glad to be home. She gave him a welcoming hug. He could hardly wait to share his thoughts with her. She served him a heaping bowl of warmed-up stew and waited for him to get satisfied and comfortable. They shared a piece of pie and coffee. The children sleeping soundly in the upstairs room snored away. Sarah Ann felt a conversation coming on.

"Tell me about your trip," she said.

"I took the boys down on the train. They looked at the Columbia River and the Cascades and saw up close some of the things they had studied in school. It rained on our arrival in Portland. I hired a man to take us to Mrs. Jones's boarding house, which is in the same block as the academy. She houses six or eight boys who go to school there. Les and Lee have a room to share with two beds and two study desks. They have to share a highboy dresser. Mrs. Jones furnishes breakfast and supper. The students prepare or buy their own food at noon. The kitchen is available as long as they clean up after themselves. One shelf in one of her iceboxes is designated for boarders' food. I tried not to chuckle about the cleaning up part. Those two have been taught better, but they were never much to clean up without being told."

Sarah Ann gave a little chuckle as she remembered how many times she had told those boys what to do. "Did they get registered for classes?"

"There wasn't a big choice. First years take a general beginning course to start with, learn to study, give the teachers an idea of what they already know. Then, after Christmas, they choose something of special interest such as the History of Oregon, Native Plants and Animals, or Business in America. What do you think those boys will pick?" asked Thomas with a twinkle.

"Well, I'm sure it won't be Business in America," answered Sarah Ann.

"I spent the night at the Imperial. The decorating looks good, almost too high class for the clientele. The manager was out so I was unable to talk over plans or profits, but there will be another chance. We may want to make a visit to the boys after they are over their homesickness."

"Were they homesick?"

"Les seemed fine, full of bravado when I saw them the next day. I didn't give Lee a chance to tear up as I made a hasty getaway to catch the train." He noticed Sarah Ann's worried look and went on to reassure her. "I'm sure they are just fine."

They sat together for a while, each thinking, feeling the warmth of sharing the couch and the dying fire in the living room. Thomas cleared his throat and Sarah Ann knew she was about to hear his latest idea or plan. "I was thinking on the drive home about the future for the other children." This was Thomas, always planning ahead.

"And just what were you thinking?"

"There is land up the river that Lee could have. That piece of property across the river that includes one pasture and the hill land could go to Les. Eventually, I picture George running the place that borders the ranch on the other side of the lane. I expect that pretty little Mary will have no trouble marrying. Then I thought about Eddie. We really have no plans for Eddie. I see he has difficulty controlling his temper. I'm afraid he'll be in trouble when he comes upon a strict schoolmaster. I kept practicing things I could say to him on the drive home. If you had been along I would have practiced them on you." Thomas was remembering his imaginary conversation with Eddie.

"You're right. I don't know what you planned to say, but we both need to take a firm hand with the boy. He scoots out of sight when he knows I'm going to reprimand him and I am less likely to follow him than I did the older children. He gets away with bad behavior. The girls don't like to challenge him because he gets mad, all red in the face, and yowls. It's not worth our time to fuss with him. That is not the correct attitude and I know it."

"We want to keep his temper at home until he learns to control it. Our job is to see he grows up to be a good citizen. First, I guess he needs to be a good citizen at home."

"You used to have a strap by the back door that was useful for rebellious boys. I think they were less troublesome after learning where it was and that it should stay on the hook at all costs."

"Ma, I guess you're right, but I have never been a person to beat a child. As you know, that strap was rarely used. If I take that route with Eddie, I'll find myself using it more with him than all the others put together."

Sarah Ann gazed at her husband. His gentle eyes and his hair that was beginning to grey said more than words about who he was. The patient man who considered his actions carefully, the man who took responsibility for his family seriously, was the man who was aging and needed to reap the rewards of his efforts. But, he was a wise man and the issue of helping Eddie control his temper was going to be addressed first thing in the morning. Thomas banked the fire and followed his wife to bed. The decision was made. Before turning in, he gave her the newspapers he had picked up in Portland.

\* \* \*

The next morning, Thomas greeted his family. "Good morning," he said, as he got a hug from each of his daughters. George stepped up and shook hands like a man. Eddie didn't know whether to hug or shake so he just sat down and drank his milk. "Eddie, what do you have to say for yourself?"

"Nothin'."

"I'd like you to come with me to the field today. We'll take the team and you can hold them for me when I get out to open gates and check things." Thomas tried to sound businesslike.

"O. K." Eddie thought something was fishy. His pa never asked him to go along.

After breakfast and the milking had been done, Thomas and Eddie drove off to check out the ranch. Sure enough, the team stomped and shook their heads when the reins were in Eddie's hands. The boy had no patience and became frightened. Thomas had to calm the team every time Eddie held the reins. It made for a slow morning for Thomas and a miserable one for Eddie. When they got back to the house for dinner, his pa said, "Never mind, Eddie. We'll go again tomorrow. You'll get the hang of it."

The boy stomped up the steps and came to the table without washing his hands. "Eddie, that basin on the porch is to be used before you eat!" His ma was on his case. Eddie believed he was the guy who never did anything right.

Things looked better after a good dinner. George and Mary invited him outside to play. The fort under the fir tree took on elegance now that Mary added her touches. Some little girl dolls took care of the house. George and Eddie took the horses their pa had carved for them off to fight the Indians again. Always victors, the boys returned around the tree ready for Mary's meal made of little berries, fir needles, and chopped up leaves. After pretending to eat, the soldiers rode off again to patrol the fort.

George seemed happy with Eddie and even let him play with his special blocks after supper. Thomas got George his blocks when he was three years old. He went to the sawmill and picked up finished pieces cut to symmetrical lengths. Some were short, some long, some triangular, and best of all, the little ones that had been turned on a router and looked like men, or castle tops, or whatever could be imagined. The blocks were kept safely in a cracker box with wheels. One could pull the box around to the place on the floor where the boys could build. The blocks must always be returned to the wagon just so, large ones on the bottom and router pieces on top. Everything fit perfectly.

"Put them away right," ordered George.

"I will. I always do!" replied Eddie.

"No you don't. You have to be told every time." When George was three his pa taught him how to put the blocks away carefully, one of those father-son bonding activities. When Eddie came along, he was just expected to follow the example and do it right. The bonding step never took place for him.

Eddie tossed the blocks in the cracker box and headed upstairs. Thomas gave Sarah Ann the look that said, "This is the time." He climbed the stairs to the boys' room and took a stern look at Eddie. "Come back and put the blocks away properly." The order was issued.

The boy's eyes grew dark and a scowl developed across his brow. "George bosses me around all the time. Those are just old blocks," growled Eddie.

"This time, George is not bossing you around. I am. I expect you to mind me and to be nice about it. Getting mad never solves a problem and you must learn that." Thomas stood waiting for a proper response. None was coming. Eddie refused to do what his pa asked. Thomas did not go to the back porch for the strap; he just removed the belt from his pant loops, put the boy over his knee and administered three sound whacks. Tears of humiliation rolled down Eddie's cheeks, but he didn't make a sound. He went down to pick up the blocks, but his anger was still seething at his unjust life. He decided when he got mad after this, it wouldn't be where his pa could see him.

"**THOMAS, I'VE BEEN** giving it some thought and I think this old leg of mine is about to give up. I've limped around for a long time and it hurts like the dickens some days. Doc Doud said about all I could do was stay off of it and see if it would heal up."

Thomas was not surprised to hear Lem's statement. He waited for his old friend and ranch hand to get his say out. "There's this little house in town next to Charity and Herman's place. I think I'd like to move in there. I've saved money all the years I've worked here and eaten Sarah Ann's good cooking. The place in town is close to Charity and she's a pretty good cook herself."

"I know that injury laid you up pretty good so I guess I'm not surprised. Things will be very different around here without you. No one else knows the place like we do. I'll need to get another hand unless you can stay until the twins get home from their school in Portland. The two of them might be worth the one of you." Both men chuckled at that statement.

"Doc says there is no hurry unless it gets to hurting more. I'll stay until the boys get here, but I think I'm only about a three quarter man anymore," Lem said.

Thomas went up to the house. "Well, Ma, I guess even your apple pies won't keep Lem with us much longer. He says he can stay until Les and Lee get home. I need to be sure the boys want to work the ranch or I'll have to find a new hand. Lem says he has saved money to move to town because we have been feeding him all these years. I think he meant that as a compliment to you."

Sarah Ann supposed so. Lem would be missed, but filling the table with just family sounded nice for a change.

The twins came home at the end of their second year term. As expected, they had finished all the school they thought necessary. One pretty young woman named Missy Dodge caught Lee's eye. She attended church regularly and taught the small children during the sermon. She wore extraordinary hats. One could not see the preacher if sitting behind Miss Dodge. Lee was more interested in seeing Miss Dodge than the preacher anyway. Lee rode to church on his own horse instead of with the family. He was seen stopping at the Dodge house on Sunday afternoons. The Dodge family played card games and constructed jigsaw puzzles Sunday afternoons. He became a welcome fourth at the games and he had a good eye for puzzles. Mrs. Dodge invited him to stay for supper on occasion. Lee found himself riding home in the dark after a day with Missy.

As everyone expected, eventually Lee asked Missy to marry him. When he talked to Mr. Dodge, he realized he had to think about his future, and it prompted him to talk to his pa. Could he work the ranch and earn enough to live on? Lee had skipped the numbers classes at the academy, so knew very little about business. Thomas wrote out on a paper what he could do for Lee and a bride. He sketched the ranchland up the river on a makeshift map.

"If you do the ranch work on this property, we can pool our resources, sell cattle together, and I will pay you with title to the land when we make a good profit. We can work together to build you a house. With luck we should be profitable in five years. So share these thoughts with Missy and see what she thinks."

Thomas had put his dream for Lee in motion. "Now we will see," he thought.

The twins could have been called "a couple of young bucks," but only Les fit the title. Lee became smitten with Missy, who kept him very much on the straight and narrow. Les rode out of town to dances. He hit the pool hall on occasion where he ran into his uncle Herman. There was no girl in town or up the valley who enticed Les. He took a couple of days to ride to Baker City. He took a couple more to ride to the Idaho Territory. Les was a restless young man. Thomas wondered if he could keep him interested in ranching or if he would have to go looking for a stranger to be his new ranch hand.

In Baker City, he met a young woman named Martha. She was the only child of Maude and Charlie Hendron. Charlie fell on hard times and Maude's many miscarriages created a sad family. Martha had dreams of a better life and Les looked like her answer. She knew his father had a good-sized spread in the Upper John Day valley. He might be her answer to the good life.

Les agreed. Impulsively, the couple married on one of his trips to Baker City. Martha had a fine-boned black horse and liked riding, so they rode to the ranch together, stopping at the Austin House for the night to break up the long trip. Only when they started down the lane did Les realize he would have to tell his father and mother what he had done, and that he had no plans for the future. He would tell them how much he loved the beautiful Martha and wait for the response.

\* \* \*

After the shock of Les and his bride, Thomas said, "Let me think about this. Why don't you take a walk down the river? Show Martha what this land is like. Gaze at Strawberry Mountain with the glacier still on it. I need some time to cogitate."

Sarah Ann took to the kitchen, her way of dealing with stressful situations. George, Mary, Eddie, and Evelyn needed feeding. She imagined only she and Thomas would have temporarily lost their appetites.

Lee knew Les had a girlfriend named Martha, but bringing her home as his wife surprised the brother. They had even spent the night at the Austin House. Lee felt a twinge of jealousy at this, as he was still waiting to marry Missy and share their promised night after the wedding.

The young people came back to the house in time for supper. Martha had seen the river bridge built by the Martin men from the logs they felled and the lumber they planed. Les had shown her the fishing holes he frequented as a youngster. They walked by the Martin school and she heard the story of his pa building the school to educate the Manwaring and Martin children. Les told about his ma's trip across the plains. Then they looked at the land on the south side of the river and saw how it was guarded by the Blue Mountains with majestic Strawberry Mountain, the highest point. The marriage, the ride, the Austin House, and the walk around the ranch had been exhilarating for Martha. Now, one look at Pa and she knew it was time to come down to earth.

Sarah Ann and Thomas had talked briefly. "I have always had plans for the boy. Now he is a man who still acts like an impulsive boy," Thomas fussed.

"What do you plan to do about it?"

"I guess I must offer him the same plan I offered to Lee. After all, they are twins deserving of the same just because they are our boys."

Sarah Ann sighed with relief. She could not bear to have unpleasantness in the house over this marriage." Where do you think they should live?"

"What do you think of offering them the bunkhouse now that Lem has moved to town?"

"Not very fancy. I imagine Martha dreamed of more, but impulse leaves one dangling."

"Done. I'll present the proposal. We will help them build a house after haying is over. I don't think they can expect more than that."

So Thomas and Les struck the bargain and Martha tried to be gracious, looking to a future that would certainly surpass the one her parents had endured.

\* \* \*

Dr. Doud had been a neighbor for several years as a single man. When he and the widow Hadley married, they built a nice house, larger than what two people needed, but Mrs. Hadley Doud had ideas of entertaining and establishing a social life for the upper valley. The house was furnished with his and hers, but the hard working people of the farms, mines and logging operations had little time for socializing. The big house went unused for the most part. The Douds decided to sell it and Doc moved his practice to the Willamette Valley. Thomas discovered he could make a good buy of the house and small piece of land that bordered his. It seemed a good answer for Les and his wife, and the family could put all their efforts into building for Lee and Missy.

Les and Martha occupied the bunkhouse for three months until the Douds moved, and then they moved over and rattled around in the big two-story house, as their furniture supply was non-existent.

"They are short of furniture." Sarah Ann gave an inquiring look at Thomas.

"They need a challenge, something to help them build character," he replied. The subject was closed. Thomas had invested all he planned to in Les's adventure of marriage.

Lem rode up to work on the new house for Lee and Missy. He wasn't much for ladders, but he knew how to build. They first built the kitchen attached to a stone storage area, the future pantry. One bedroom was built just off the dining room that was joined by a living room. A rather grand staircase led upstairs from the dining room. The bedrooms filled the upstairs. Lem insisted on the one bedroom downstairs. He said Missy could use it for sewing, but every house needing a sleeping area downstairs for when the house owners got old and couldn't climb the stairs. The fireplace in the living room and the cook stove in the kitchen provided heat. The house was finished off with a fashionable front porch with carved white pillars donated by the bride's family, just in time for the wedding. Lee and Missy received wedding gifts to help them get started. One could wonder if Martha was jealous, but not a word was said. Les told her, "When we all get to work it will be even-steven because we are twins and that's how things are."

\* \* \*

The twins had started their families. Mary and George were growing up and thinking along the same lines. Mary and Missy had been classmates and friends. When one married, it seemed the other would also.

Monty Bly moved to Prairie City and went into business next to Marsh's. He furnished dry goods to the shoppers in the valley. Fabric and thread enticed the ladies who sewed for their families. Ready-made work shirts and pants, suspenders and boots drew the men. Pioneers are frugal folks, but after fifteen years, their clothes were worn out and outgrown, so Bly's business had instant success. He spotted Mary shopping for fabric and experienced "love at first sight." A suitable courtship followed by a lovely wedding completed Thomas's dream for his daughter to marry well.

George was no lady's man and the opportunity to marry did not present itself. He convinced Thomas his education was fine for ranching. "Eighth grade is enough," he said with authority. He believed in advanced education, just not for himself. So he became his pa's right hand man, haying, rustling cattle, venturing into the purebred business, where they kept a given name for each cow, recorded her calving record, and weeded the herd to make it strong. George showed a talent for record-keeping and a talent for building as well as doing the rest of the ranch chores without complaint. He helped Les build some furniture for his house. Generally, the little brother whom the twins had tortured in their youth, proved to be helpful to them in many ways. George and Thomas worked two ranches together, one on either side of the lane. Their herds mingled while Les and Lee kept theirs separate.

Across the lane from the Martin School stood a deserted house that the original homesteaders had built. Alice Larson, one of Andy Larson's daughters, was hired to teach in the school. The Grant County Board of Education filled the positions for the one-room schoolhouses throughout the valley. Alice finished studies at the academy in Portland before she was hired. George decided to fix up the homesteader's place and offer it to her as housing. It sat on his property and he wanted to help everyone else get educated. Alice lived with her mother up the river. They were trying to keep the place her father had homesteaded, but it was proving hard work for two women, as Alice's sister had married the previous year and moved to her husband's place.

"Hello there, Alice," George greeted her. He and Alice were the same age and would have been schoolmates in town if George had not stopped his formal education after eighth grade.

"Hello, George, how are you today?" asked the new teacher.

"Just fine, thanks. I stopped to see if you had any needs for school."

"I have the necessary books, class records that I must keep for the county, and enough desks. It looks as if school is ready. The outhouse has been disinfected and moved to its new location. The parents of the children who go to the Martin School do a nice job of keeping things up. We closed the Larson School after Papa died because the attending families just didn't do the upkeep work." Alice had not meant to tell all of this to George, but out it came.

"The little house across the street is empty. I'd be glad to clean it up for you to stay in." George just made an offer that could mean a lot of work.

"Let me think on that for a bit. Staying close to school would be handier than riding down every day."

As George was about to leave, Alice thought maybe he could help her move a bookcase she wanted in a different location. "George, could you help me slide that old bookcase over to the other wall?"

The bookcase was tall, a big job for a short man. Alice was tall for a woman, so together they made a good bookcase moving team. He pushed the bottom half as she steadied the top. George took his leave and headed down the lane whistling *Annie Laurie* for no particular reason he knew.

\* \* \*

Alice took a liking to teaching. She demanded a quiet classroom and good work. Her penmanship set an exemplary example for her students and she did not accept sloppy work. One of her favorite students was little Evelyn Martin, who was a dainty first grader. Who could not be taken with a dainty first grader dressed in the pretty outfits her mother made for her? Already she showed a love of books and a propensity for numbers. Her brother, Eddie, provided the school ground protection she needed at recess. Little Evelyn enjoyed all the good things in life, a benefit of being the last born in a family whose parents were successful ranchers. Alice knew Evelyn's ma was well read and interested in the current news, especially the women's rights issues. Alice felt a kindred spirit, having been raised by the most forward thinking man in the valley. She did not applaud her father's teaching, but some of it stuck with her. Alice attended church because everyone *should*, but she questioned what she heard although she avoided discussing her ideas. She watched her father lose favor with his neighbors because of his thoughts, which he expressed all too freely. George kept the little house in good repair for her, so she only rode up to see her mother on weekends and during school holidays.

Eddie Martin proved to be a discipline challenge. When he became frustrated with his work, he would rip up his papers. He strived for perfect papers and was unable to accept less. The work he did earned 80% or better, but he was only content with 93% or better. Someone had stressed the importance of grades and Eddie took that someone very seriously. Thomas had decided Eddie's success lay in serious studies, maybe even work beyond the ranch. Thomas set goals for Eddie. Thomas thought Eddie's temperament might be suited to some other business, not the meat market. George had taken an interest in it and was actually doing a fine job of running it as well as working the ranch. Eddie read his ma's newspapers.

*Maybe I could be a boxer. I couldn't make heavy weight, but there are other divisions. Maybe I could race horses. I'm a good rider. I just need a faster horse. Maybe I could throw baseballs at a fair or play on a baseball team. Maybe I'm just a dreamer, but I'll show Pa.* Miss Larson saw that Eddie was a dreamer, but her job was to teach reading, writing, and numbers. Children's dreams belonged elsewhere, not in the classroom.

\* \* \*

Les went bird hunting. Creeping through the brush beside the river, noting the calling cards left by big birds, he quietly stalked the bank looking for wild turkeys roosting in the trees. *They are not the most tender birds,* he thought to himself, *but my ma can do wonders if I can just bag a couple of them.* Snow had fallen and melted, making November's typical muddy mess. His right foot slipped into the icy water, soaking his boot and wool shock. *Get a bird before my right foot freezes,* he told himself. Just then, he spotted three turkeys in the tall chokecherry tree. In summer, the family picked chokecherries from this huge bush grown into a tree. Sarah Ann created a special syrup for pancakes from the chokecherries. Today, the tree would provide a Thanksgiving bird. Les raised the shotgun to his shoulder, aimed and shot. Hooray! One big bird fell dead to the bank. Another wounded one fell in the river. *It won't get away*, thought Les as he tromped into the very cold water. *Just as well to have two wet feet as one.*

He arrived back at the main house with two wet boots and two wild turkeys. Sarah Ann could see the Thanksgiving menu would be set around turkey this year. Les removed his boots and socks and put them by the stove to dry. Sarah Ann found an old pair of Thomas's socks for him to wear while he went to the porch to clean the birds. She boiled a huge pot of water to scald the ugly critters in so Les could get all the pin feathers off. They hung the birds by their feet on the porch, where they would stay cold until cooking time. The full day's work ended; Les put on his dry boots and socks and headed across the fields toward Martha.

# APPLE TIME
# SEPTEMBER 1890

**THE WHOLE FAMILY** gathered to pick apples. Sarah Ann and the girls dumped the apples from the picking buckets into bushel baskets and apple boxes. Every man climbed a tree to harvest the fruit.

"Ma, are you wool gathering?" yelled Thomas from across the orchard. Sarah Ann looked up to see the twins both waiting for her to get their buckets and dump them.

"I guess I was. Sorry." She wondered what Thomas would say if he knew the thoughts that were running through her mind. Admiration for Abigail Duniway made her want to go to Portland with Thomas and hear Abigail's speech at the rally honoring Susan B. Anthony.

*Back in 1869 when Thomas and I were married, Joaquin Miller's wife, Minnie, was known for her ideas about women's rights. She had a very small following in Canyon City where she and Judge Miller lived. People knew of her education and sharp wit. The life she led in this rural area as the wife of the county judge was not what she had signed on for when she met Joaquin. He was a dashing adventurer and poet who courted her on his trips up and down the Oregon coast. After some time in California, he passed back up the coast and swept her off her feet with his swaggering ways. She believed in him, knowing he had a degree in the law. The future looked promising for her. I followed her with some interest because Judge Miller had performed our wedding ceremony and Mrs. Miller had been present.*

*News of a split between the couple came, accompanied by the tale of Joaquin's escapades in Northern California where he had lived with a remote Indian tribe for two years, had taken a young native woman as a bride and had fathered a child. Deserting his Indian family, he rode up the coast and stopped in Reedsport to again court Minnie. She was not privy to the two years spent as an Indian husband. One of his old cronies from that time looked him up in Canyon City and let the story of Pretty Dove escape his lips. Mrs. Miller packed her belongings and left the very next day. Blessed with a good education, she established herself in Portland and championed the women's causes in a good loud voice. The folks in the valley followed her with interest. The judge left the area to do his lawyering elsewhere and finally to write his famous poetry of the Sierras.*

*Abigail Duniway's newspaper, "The New Northwest," was a forum for others such as Minnie Miller. Abigail's husband was injured in a runaway accident in 1862 and could only do light work. She became the breadwinner of the family. Had she had the luxury of remaining home to care for her family, one wonders if she would have taken up the cause of suffrage.*

*I'm surprised I know so much about the ladies and the topic. I must have been harboring a secret interest in this topic for some time. I think I need to infuse my children with these ideas, especially the girls. When I get in the house, I'm going to write to Amy about the voting rights for women. I can't imagine that Stubble would be in favor of giving his wife a vote.*

*Enough! Get back to the apple orchard. That's where we'll get enough money for me to make a trip to Portland next year.*

# 1896

**SARAH ANN PUSHED** the pot of chicken stock to the back of the stove where it would stay warm but not boil until she brought it forward to drop in the dumplings. Eddie was late for supper.

"Pa, have you seen Eddie yet? School was out two hours ago," she asked.

"No, I went ahead and did his chores. If he knew we were having chicken and dumplings, he'd be on time," said Thomas.

"That's what I was thinking," said Sarah Ann. "I was looking forward to seeing the comments on that paper the teacher was grading."

"You know, he felt picked on because he had to redo that paper. Mr. Page is pretty 'old school' in his thinking and seems to want his students to think the same way," fussed Sarah Ann.

They heard a horse coming across the lot. "It's not Eddie. He would have gone straight to the barn," said Thomas.

Clint Evert rode up, out of breath and red faced, and shouted, "Is Eddie home yet?"

"What's wrong?" asked Thomas.

"Eddie stayed after school to argue with Mr. Page about his paper, the one he needed a passing grade on to earn his diploma. They got pretty loud. Mr. Page shoved Eddie away. Everybody knows you don't shove Eddie Martin. He punched Page in the nose. The teacher swung back and it was one helluva fight, excuse my language, Mrs. Martin," reported Clint.

Just then Eddie's horse was spotted on the lane with the rider slumped over the side, hanging onto the saddle horn.

Thomas and Clint helped Eddie from the saddle and brought him into the house.

"Evelyn, get some clean towels and washrags and the good bar soap," ordered Sarah Ann. She proceeded to wash the wounds on his face and hands, some still bleeding and others caked with dirt and dried blood. Sarah Ann was gentle but thorough. She instructed Evelyn to chip some ice from the block in the icebox to apply to the worst of the bruises.

Clint excused himself when he saw Eddie looked as if he would recover, saying, "I need to get home or my mom will be worried." When he departed, Sarah Ann knew he would be the one to spread the gossip about this unfortunate fight.

"Eddie, what happened?" asked his ma.

"Let the boy tell us in his own time," suggested Thomas. He wanted the truth, not a made up tale to satisfy his ma's questioning.

Eddie sat up and managed to share some of the chicken and dumplings. "Mr. Page did not like the report. He said my sources were not credible. He said I would not get my diploma. I told him it was not fair. He got really steamed up because I questioned his right to judge me. He tried to shove me out the door and followed me out as he pushed. I hit him and before I knew it, we had a big fight. I won. He was flat on the ground and bleeding when I left," Eddie explained.

"I suggest we all try to get a night's sleep and decide what is to be done in the morning." As usual, Thomas was the voice of reason. Sarah Ann was filled with silent worry and knew she would not get the suggested sleep.

The next morning, Clint returned at a gallop. "They dragged Mr. Page to the doctor last night, but he is dead. The whole thing is the talk of the town. The sheriff will be coming up from Canyon City to look into it," reported Clint.

Eddie, more frightened than ever, filled a backpack and rode off to be out of reach of the law. His parents stood helpless as he left. There was no stopping him from running. He stopped at the Flasher place up Strawberry Creek and spent the next night. They also tried to convince him not to run.

The teacher did not die, but there was no way to let Eddie know. A story in the newspaper wrongly reported the death, so Eddie put as much space as he could between Prairie City and himself.

Three months passed. Eddie wrote his family a letter to say he was well but not to look for him. There was no return address. Sarah Ann couldn't help thinking that a second man in her life had run away. This time it was a son, not a husband. Broken hearts never mend completely. Sarah Ann's heart now had two big cracks, but it was held together by the love of one strong committed man who would never run: her wonderful Thomas.

Without Eddie at home, Sarah Ann felt an emptiness that could not be filled. Thomas tried to bring her comfort. They read together and shared their good thoughts. They ignored the subject of Eddie. People talked about the fight and about his disappearance. Sarah Ann did not like being the subject of gossip, so she avoided going to town.

Evelyn's autograph book, the purple velvet one she received as a Christmas gift, held a treasured page, *"To my little Sister, Evelyn. Be a good girl, Have a good life, One of these days, You'll be a good wife. Your Brother, Eddie."* Not a very original greeting, but there it sat on the page in his own handwriting, and the rare tears rolled down the cheeks of all who read it.

After a time friends finally stopped asking, "Have you heard from Eddie?"

"No, nothing yet," was always Sarah Ann's answer. Of course if the family did hear they couldn't admit it.

Sarah Ann devoted her time to rearing Evelyn to be a lady, being sure she was well read and doing well with her studies. Evelyn went with them on their trips to Portland, where they stayed in the well-decorated Imperial Hotel. The part interest in the establishment paid off dividends, another of Pa's wise business decisions. They investigated schools in the Portland area. Evelyn decided on Holms Business College. She knew a friend who attended there, Letty Sharp, who used to live in Prairie City. Letty's brother was always willing to squire the girls around when the Martins went to Portland. Evelyn considered his attention an added benefit to the business college. Arrangements were made for Evelyn to attend in the fall of '98.

On the home front, George made a serious move. He asked Alice Larson, the school marm at the Martin School, to become his wife. The Martins approved because she was well educated and would do a lot toward George's success as a rancher.

Sarah Ann told George, "Good choice, Son."

Alice wore a pure silk veil fastened with a large covered button on the top. The veil split halfway down to fall on either side of the fashionable bustle of the creamy white dress. Her matching shoes with their hourglass-shaped heels came from the St. Louis catalogue at the cost of $2.00. Thomas thought that cost was too much for shoes she would not wear again, but he was not paying for them so he kept quiet, except to Sarah Ann.

The minister performed the ceremony at Mrs. Larson's house. Alice's sister, Clara, was the bridesmaid. After the official documents were signed, the couple took a buggy to the Austin House for their first night. After a couple of days they came home to the house across from the school, on George's property. Alice quit teaching at the end of the school year and devoted herself to being a rancher's wife.

# LETTERS AND DIARIES
# 1897

*My Dear Amy,*

*It excites me to know that you will be allowed to vote for our next President. The residents of Idaho Territory, few as they are, must be very forward looking. I have wanted to see women's rights put forth for some time, ever since my trip to New York. I could see the coming tide and I had a personal breakthrough in my thinking at that time. I do hope you and Stubble continue to live on the Idaho side of the river, because this privilege would be lost to you if you move to the Oregon side of the ferry. J.J. and Lincoln could live on the Oregon side where it would make no difference. Men vote everywhere. Treasure what Idaho offers you and don't let Stubble move you.*

*We have made arrangements for Evelyn in Portland next year. George and Alice are settled in their house. Knowing George, he will be building-on and remodeling to make it perfect for his bride.*

*Sadly, we know nothing of Eddie. We must all keep his safety in our prayers. I hope somewhere he has seen the newspaper retraction that Mr. Page recovered. If he always believes he killed another human being, it will affect the kind of man he becomes. I guess by now he is a man, but I will only be able to remember him as a hotheaded boy who was sorry for his actions in the end.*

*Greetings to you and your husband and children. Best wishes for a peaceful holiday season.*

*Lovingly,*

*Ma*

**SARAH ANN** read *The Story of America* by Elia Peattie. He claimed the greatest popular novel of the time was *Uncle Tom's Cabin*. Sarah Ann was not sure she agreed. The nation was a hundred and twenty-five years old and it amazed her to realize she had lived for over sixty years of that time. People were looking toward a new century. It would be difficult to remember to write 1900 instead of 1800.

Thomas brought home some stronger glasses for Sarah Ann. They helped some with her reading. She hated to admit that she did not feel well on many days. Thomas was aware and asked what was wrong. Sarah Ann was not sure so she made an appointment with the new doctor who replaced Dr. Doud. She asked Mary to go with her, "I don't want to go alone," stated Sarah Ann.

The doctor was not sure what the trouble was. He gave her some powders to take for indigestion and suggested a mild diet.

"I think he has the right idea as I am feeling better," Sarah Ann told Thomas.

She began writing her thoughts in a diary:

*Spring is upon us and that is another reason to feel better. We look forward to another profitable year with the cattle, haying, and harvesting the apples. I think an apple tree has more to offer than any plant. Thomas put in this orchard over thirty years ago and it is still producing wonderful apples. Right now, in April, the trees are beginning to blossom, white touched with pink, like miniature clouds that match the spring sky.*

*Buttercups on the hill are the most glorious we have had. Thomas took me in the buggy for a ride just to see them hiding in the bunch grass. Finally, I seem to have time to enjoy these small pleasures. Another day we walked up the river with our poles and brought home trout for breakfast. Evelyn does the housework and a great deal of the work I used to do without a complaint. Thomas says he'll get me some extra help when Evelyn goes to business school. I do love this thoughtful man.*

*Sept. 1898*

*Thomas and I have decided to take Evelyn to school. It is a long three-day trip, but we will stop at the little hotel in Dayville near where the Stewarts live. They are old time pioneers in the lower part of the valley. Then we will stay at the Ochoco Inn, another notable stop in central Oregon in the town of Prineville, an area settled by the Prines, also early pioneers. The drive on the south side of Mt. Hood puts us in touch with extraordinary scenery that I have always wanted to see. The main reason we are doing this is to take me to a more experienced doctor. The stomach pains have grown worse and I need some relief.*

*After depositing Evelyn at business college, September 20, with many hugs and promises to write, Thomas took me to St. Vincent Hospital. The examining doctor shook his head and wore a worried look on his face. He determined my trouble was gallbladder stones. He suggested surgery to remove them. Thomas and I were frightened, but we decided to risk the operation. I have read enough about new medical practices to know they are risky. I also knew that many antiquated procedures are no longer in use. The danger from infections is still the worst part of surgery.*

*I was very thankful that my husband has been successful and could afford to provide the best care available in Portland. He was at my side beforehand and I knew he would be there when the surgery was over.*

*I felt very nauseous. A nurse held a silver colored dish beside me and I vomited into it. I hated having Thomas watch all if this, but I was glad he was there to comfort me. Between vomits, the doctor came to report a successful surgery. He had some minute stones to show me that he had removed along with my gallbladder. The incision down the middle of my stomach was sore to touch and he said to allow two weeks for it to heal. It was a long time for Thomas to be away from the ranch. He said not to worry. He sold the team and wagon so we could take the train home to Baker City. Then our ride home in a wagon was much shorter.*

*We made it home before the end of October. This is my favorite season. Many leaves still hang on the trees with a bit of color enhancing the crisp days. The boys and their wives cared for the orchard while we were gone, stored the apples, canned applesauce and sold the small surplus to Marsh's store. I am sighing and thinking how life goes on without us if we are taken off track*

*January 30, 1899*

*I have spent the past three months recovering and trying to be my old self. But, I know my time is growing short. I have happily lived with a lie since my trip to New York. My decision is still the same. No one will ever know the truth of the desertion by my first husband. I have helped my daughters grow up to be strong and independent. They will never be devastated by a man. I have shared the treasure of Thomas Martin, the man who committed himself to me for life, for the life that will soon end for me.*

*This paragraph written in this journal to clarify my thoughts will be ripped out and burned in the cook stove under the left hand burner which I will lift with the short black poker as I have done for nearly thirty years, when I stoke the coals, heat the coils, and boil the water for our morning oatmeal.*

Sarah Ann headed for the kitchen to fix Thomas his usual breakfast for after he finished the morning chores. This was the day she was going to burn the diary entries, to burn up the lie, to begin the new century on a positive note. She reached for the poker to open the firebox.

Thomas came in from the barn to find her on the floor, unable to speak or move.

# THE OBITUARY

**SARAH ANN HUNT** Manwaring Martin passed from this earthly life on February 1, 1899. She was born in Long Island, New York to James Hunt and Ann Manwaring Hunt, October 7, 1837. Her marriage to Cody Manwaring ended when he was captured by Indians during the wagon trip west known as the Manwaring Train, which arrived in the John Day Valley in 1869. Sarah Ann married Thomas H. Martin on February 5, 1870.

Well-loved by her family and neighbors, her many talents included tailoring, cooking and all other talents a mother and rancher's wife must possess. Those who knew her appreciated her straightforward manner and her honesty. Her devotion to the Methodist Church and her study of the Bible helped her create a wonderful home and raise a moral family.

In her later years, Mrs. Martin fostered an interest in women's rights and suffrage. Her suggestion was instrumental in the change in Oregon's law that requires young women to be sixteen years of age to legally marry.

Mrs. Martin underwent surgery in Portland last year for a bad gallbladder. Recovery from that major surgery slowed her activities and she lacked the strength to survive the recurring infection that plagued her.

Survivors include her husband of twenty-nine years, Thomas Martin; sons, John and Lincoln Manwaring, Lester, Leland, George and Edwin Martin; daughters, Amy Stubble, Mary Bly and Evelyn Martin.

Services held at the Prairie City Methodist Church were followed by burial in the Prairie City Cemetery in the Martin plot next to her mother-in-law. The rare warm February day found many friends of the family attending both services.

Wild buttercups could be seen peeking through the grass where the snow had melted.

Made in the USA
Las Vegas, NV
20 September 2022